"Are we as bad as all that?" Sally asked gently.

"No," Karen said. "It was just that I realized you were all Peggy's friends."

"Only because you always took such a back seat," Sarah protested. "Nobody could really get to know you."

"Well, Peggy couldn't stand any competition, could she?" Sally asked.

Karen felt the faint tug of that old requirement to defend Peggy against the charge of egocentricity which, if it had some justice in it, was usually prompted by jealousy of Peggy's good looks, money, and charm. It was no longer necessary for Karen to display that steady loyalty. If she hadn't learned to live alone, she had learned to live without Peggy.

Reluctant as she was to have these two in her house, prying at the edge of her loneliness, what they had just revealed to her gave her new confidence. Then, as she lay in her own bed, listening to the quiet sounds of their lovemaking punctuated by the popping and collapsing fire, she felt her defenses burning away like her very skin. Even here in her own house, she was alone in the cold and dark while two people she hardly knew usurped the center.

After the Fire

by Jane Rule

Macmillan of Canada
A Division of Canada Publishing Corporation
Toronto, Ontario, Canada
1989

Canadian Cataloguing in Publication Data
Rule, Jane, date.
After the fire

ISBN 0-7715-9615-4

1. Title.

PS8535.U43A73 1989   C813.54   C89-094306-0
PR9199.3.R84A73 1989

Edited by Katherine V. Forrest
Typeset by Sandi Stancil

The poem "Rumination" by Richard Eberhart, appearing on pages 237–238 is from COLLECTED POEMS 1930–1986 by Richard Eberhart. Copyright © 1988 by Richard Eberhart. Reprinted by permission of Oxford University Press, Inc.

Appearing on page 41 are twelve lines, three stanzas, from A. E. Housman's "To an Athlete Dying Young," are reprinted from THE COLLECTED POEMS OF A. E. HOUSMAN, Copyright © 1939, 1940, 1965 by Holt, Rinehart and Winston, Inc. Copyright © 1967, 1968 by Robert E. Symons. Reprinted by permission of Henry Holt and Company, Inc.

The poem on pages 193–194 is by Emily Dickinson and is reprinted from THE COLLECTED POEMS OF EMILY DICKINSON.

Macmillan of Canada
A Division of Canada Publishing Corporation
Toronto, Ontario, Canada

Printed in the United States of America.

WORKS BY JANE RULE

For Helen

Chapter I

The fire had bloomed into the winter night before the fire truck could get there, skidding through the slush, spewing out mud from the deep potholes of the dirt road. Behind it came the old water truck, even more slowly, and behind that a line of vehicles that might have been resurrected from the wrecking yard for the occasion.

"Christ! Do you think Dickie's still in there?" Homer, the driver of the fire truck, shouted to the young woman sitting next to him.

Karen Tasuki didn't reply. This was her first real

fire. The noise, the heat, the beauty of it amazed, dazed her.

"Come on!" Homer shouted, already halfway out his door.

Then she was on the ground, stumbling, fumbling, with half a dozen other people, who might never have been at all those weekly practices, so routine, so slow-motion and silly without slush and mud and darkness and roaring light.

Their chief was not among them, had taken the night ferry across to the mainland, someone said. Whoever was supposed to take charge in his place didn't know it. People shouted conflicting directions as if they should form competing teams, play tug-of-war with the hose or knock each other down with the spray of water.

"This is ludicrous!" Karen muttered.

"Don't waste the fucking water on the house!" someone shouted. "Keep those trees from going!"

"Stand back! The roof's about to go."

Karen looked up from her length of hose and saw the neat rows of shingles faint into the fire. The only shape left now was the chimney. Even if they'd known what they were doing, there had never been a chance of saving the house or anyone or anything in it. At practice they had been told as much. Oh, they were supposed to try, but all they could hope to accomplish was to keep such a fire from spreading to the trees or outbuildings.

The hose, trained now on the trees nearest the house, suddenly died in their hands. They had used up the supply in the water truck. Cars had to be moved before it could be turned around and sent back the slow two miles to the storage tank at the fire hall.

While they waited, there wasn't much to do but stamp out the little fires started from the embers and sparks which fell like seeds and sprouted afresh if they lighted on anything but the melting snow.

"Thank God there's no wind," Homer said, taking out a cigarette, cupping a match in his large hands.

The tiny flame restored Karen for a moment to the little illusion she had had of fire. So she would confront a tidal flood with no greater understanding than she'd gained from a dripping tap. What had her father said to her? "What you sadly lack is an education for catastrophe." He hadn't meant fire practice either, but before the fact — that practicing was nothing but a lesson in futility, in helplessness. She should be back at the hall with the older women, making coffee and sandwiches.

"Did anybody phone Dickie's mother?" Homer asked.

"We don't even know if he's in there," Adam answered in a protest which reflected his friendship with Dickie.

"What's left of him is in there. Where else would he be? There's his truck."

"He wasn't in that good shape when he left the pub tonight," Karen offered.

Just about four hours ago by now. Dickie John could be a surly drunk, hard to cut off at the bar, impossible to drive home. She had cut him off half an hour before closing time, but somebody had probably bought him another drink.

"Was Red with him?" Homer asked.

"No, she didn't come in all evening," Karen said.

None of them was doing anything useful now. They had to stand, waiting and watching the fire burn itself out.

"Dickie hasn't been hanging around with Red for a couple of weeks now," said Rat, a young man with a gentle face blurred with a need for sleep.

"Must be a first for Dickie, her telling him to bugger off," Adam said, friend but also rival of the subject of their conversation.

"Do you really think the poor bastard's in there?" Rat asked.

"Look, there's no point in all of us hanging around. Rat, you've got a baby to keep you up. Why don't you give Karen here a lift back to the hall? Adam, it's going to be a hell of a short night for you, too," Homer suggested.

"I'm staying," Adam said.

"Well, Riley, how about you?"

"Yeah, okay," Riley said, looking as if his own evening's entertainment was only now wearing off badly.

Karen, aware she'd been given no choice, hadn't the will to protest. The end of the drama was going to be charred bones and ashes. She wouldn't cry, but she might vomit up her dinner.

"Maybe you should phone Dickie's mother," Homer suggested.

Before Karen could question the wisdom of that suggestion, all their attention turned to the returning water truck. They moved with new competence, grateful for something to do, though it was nothing now but playing those few hundred gallons of water on the already dying fire.

4

"Come on," Rat said to Karen. "Let's get out of here."

When they had settled in his old pickup, Karen said, "Do you really think Dickie's mother should be told, before they know for sure, I mean?"

"They know," Rat said quietly and then burst out, "What a bunch of fucking clowns!"

Inclined to agree with him but wanting to comfort, Karen said, "It was too late anyway."

"It always bloody well is," Rat said tiredly. "But why didn't Homer take charge from the beginning?"

"He only knows how to drive the fire truck," Karen said.

"Hell, he's been around forever, lived on this island all his fucking fifty years. He should have learned *something*!"

They traveled the rest of the way in silence.

"I guess there will be coffee and sandwiches," Karen said as she got out of the truck at the fire hall where she'd left her own car.

"I got to get home. I'm asleep on my feet," Rat said. "But . . . thank the ladies."

Homer's wife, Jane, Henrietta Hawkins, and the silly Milly Forbes were there, sitting around a table, drinking tea. Nobody had sampled the large ham, turkey, and egg sandwiches that sat on a plate underneath a film of Saran Wrap.

"Well?" They all turned to Karen.

"It's pretty well over. They're using the second truck of water just to damp it all down. There'll be nothing left but the chimney."

"Have they found Dickie?" Henrietta asked.

"Not yet," Karen answered. "They want me to call his mother."

"I'll do that," Henrietta said, her old face both resolute and kind.

"That poor woman!" Milly Forbes said and began to cry.

Homer's wife said, "Have a sandwich. You must be exhausted, out there working beside the men."

"I didn't do much," Karen said, knowing she should take what was offered, but nausea overcame her manners.

"You get along home to bed," Henrietta said. "You've done your share."

Karen turned gratefully away, but, once she was seat-belted into her car, she wished she had not left that human company. In the year she'd been on this little island, she had learned nothing about the one thing she had come to learn: how to live alone.

Instead, she had filled all her waking hours with any people she could find. She not only worked at the ticket booth for the ferries but also was a waitress at the local pub, rationalizing two jobs because she was saving to buy a place of her own. The thought of buying a house to live in by herself was even more daunting than returning to the little beach cottage she had rented for the winter months.

The light on the porch gave a false sense of welcome, but at least inside there were mute signs of other people's tastes. At least, she wasn't banished from their furniture. Karen was grateful, too, that she didn't have to light a fire to keep warm. She simply had to turn up the thermostat on the electric heater. Tonight even the heater felt suspect. She checked to be sure no window curtain or stray scrap of paper was anywhere near it.

Why was there that peculiar smell of smoke? She

6

hadn't been home to bother with a hearth fire for over a week. Then Karen realized she herself was the source. Her clothes, her hair smelled of cedar smoke; it didn't have the stale sweet tar smell she brought home from an evening at the pub which at least was human, if unhealthy. What she smelled now was sudden death.

Karen didn't want to think about Dickie John or what was left of him. Nor did she want to think of Homer who, however incompetent, probably did recognize a charred body when he saw one. Surely they wouldn't let Dickie's mother see that. Karen remembered the body bags carried on the fire truck, objects of macabre humor until tonight.

"I'll have to resign," Karen said aloud.

It wasn't a bad habit she'd formed but a deliberate exercise because she couldn't stand hours alone without the sound of a human voice. The radio helped, but it was not the same as a human voice right there in the room with her. She explained it to herself as keeping herself company, and therefore she was apt to carry on a conversation.

"You can't resign after your first real fire."

"Why not?"

"What happens when the next woman wants to try it?"

"Maybe I'm finding out I'm a R.E.A.L. woman after all."

"I thought you were learning not to be a coward."

"Oh, damn it! I'm going to wash my hair."

In the shower, Karen suddenly thought of Red. How would she find out about Dickie? Probably from one of the sandwich-making women. Red cleaned for both Henrietta and Milly. Let it be Henrietta — Hen, as people called her — who had such mortal good sense. Would people blame Red? Say Dickie was drinking so much because she'd dropped him?

Dickie, like Homer, was island grown, and most people, including his mother, treated him like a boy rather than the full-grown man he was. *Dickie.* What twenty-five-year-old with any self-respect would allow people to call him by such a name? Well, Dickie was such a hotshot, driving his great big lumber truck, showing off muscles still more impressive than his incipient beer belly, bragging about his collection of "pussy" — Karen had pictured pelts of pubic hair on his wall and flinched — being called *Dickie* didn't bother him.

It had surprised Karen when, several months ago, Red had turned up with Dickie at the pub. He didn't seem her type, if she had a type. Nobody seemed to know much about Red, except that she'd arrived on the island about four years ago and for practically nothing had rented a primitive little cabin with no electricity or running water. She made what money she did by cleaning for people and otherwise kept pretty much to herself.

Drying her dark, straight hair, Karen wondered where Red, whose hair was as dark as her own, had got that name. She wondered, too, how Red would feel about Dickie. She must have slept with him; Dickie didn't hang around with women for any other reason. His friends were male. Karen had loathed Dickie, but even her physical revulsion tonight had been tinged with a small but pure pity, which transferred now to the sight of her own flesh.

She remembered reading in the training manual

about the skin as an organ, how it had turned her image of her own body inside out. This thin, pliable, fragile layer of cells was the body's only protection against such a thing as fire, *that* fire, but even the flickering flame of Homer's match or a cup of boiling water . . .

Her hair was clean and dry. She got into the bed she had left several hours before and tried to sleep, but the odor of smoke still rose from the clothes she had left on the chair.

"I'll wash them tomorrow night," Karen said aloud before she remembered that she had decided not to talk in the dark.

Milly Forbes, exhausted from her sandwich-making of the night before, was still asleep when Red knocked on her kitchen door. Milly saw no one, not even a maid, before she had done her face.

"Come in," she called, and, when she heard the door open and then close, "Put on the coffee, will you, Red? I'm just dressing."

But the ten minutes she took were devoted to her make-up. Even in that time Milly could take ten years off her carefully tended face. But looking thirty-five rather than forty-five was still over-the-hill, as her late husband (he wasn't dead; she only liked to think him so) had pointed out to her some years ago.

Still in a pale blue robe the color of her eyes, Milly felt dressed enough to go to the kitchen for coffee, whose fragrance told her it was just ready.

Red was getting the vacuum cleaner out of the

back closet, her buttocks Milly's only view of her, surprisingly broad for a girl so thin, with no breasts at all, shaped like one of those fertility symbols, except that she had a head, which now rose up and turned to Milly.

"Good morning," Milly said.

"Good morning," Red replied.

"Better have a cup of coffee before you start," Milly suggested.

"Later."

"Now," Milly decided, pouring two cups. "Have you heard about the fire?"

"Fire?"

"Dickie John's place, burned to the ground with him in it."

"Dickie?"

"They said he must have been dead drunk."

Red sat down abruptly and reached out for her cup of coffee. Milly tried to read her always unsatisfactorily passive face, dark bangs obscuring her forehead, eyelids that dropped like shades over dark eyes which told nothing, a mouth natural in repose. It was Red's mouth, soft as a child's, which made Milly suspect she was younger than she let on.

"Wasn't he, for a while, somebody you . . ."

Red shrugged. "He drank too much."

"Was he . . . unhappy?"

"No. Mad when he didn't get his way is all," Red said.

"Good-looking men get spoiled," Milly said.

"Do you think he's good-looking?" Red asked.

"Oh, very. Dickie's always been good-looking. I can remember him as just a tot when Forbes and I used to come over for weekends. That gorgeous curly hair! He had bedroom eyes as a four-year-old."

"Bedroom eyes?"

"It's just an expression," Milly said.

"He was starting to get fat."

"His father was a big man," Milly said. "Died in an accident, too, in a boat. He wasn't many years older than Dickie."

"Who's told his mother?" Red asked.

"Hen went to Sadie. She'll take it hard, poor woman." Milly's tears rose again, a practiced pity for herself and her own losses easy to extend to all the others hurt, deserted, dead.

"Excuse me," Red said, and she moved off quickly to the bathroom.

Milly could hear her retching and felt satisfaction at getting a clear reaction. Red wasn't heartless after all.

"Are you all right?" she asked when Red came back even paler than usual.

"Fine now," Red said. "Sometimes I just can't drink coffee."

"That Jap girl with the blue eyes . . ." Milly began.

"Karen," Red said firmly.

"She was so pale she was white last night. You know she goes out with the fire crew?"

"I heard that."

"Well, she's learned her lesson. I don't know what's wrong with girls these days, thinking they can do anything a man does."

"Some of us have to," Red said, by now busying herself with the vacuum cleaner.

11

"You don't. She doesn't," Milly said. "There's nothing wrong with either one of you a little make-up and some attention to what you wear wouldn't cure."

"Cure seems to me worse than the problem," Red said.

"Well, you're all a mystery to me," Milly said, a comment addressed to an empty room because Red had left it.

It was the longest conversation Milly had ever had with Red in the three years Red had worked for her. Milly didn't approve of women who made confidantes of their help. She didn't have to pay for someone to talk to. But she'd sometimes felt that Red was a real miser with gossip; she must hear something occasionally, cleaning for people.

Even Hen, who had trained Red herself, knew nothing about her.

"All I know, Milly," Henrietta had said, "is that she came to me after I put up a notice on the board for someone to help me when Hart was so sick and I didn't want to have to put him in hospital any sooner than necessary. She said she didn't know the first thing about keeping house, but, if I'd teach her, she wouldn't ask for money until I thought she was worth it. When I asked her how old she was, she said, if I asked her questions like that, she'd have to lie to me, and she didn't want to lie to me. So I just didn't ask her about herself."

Red hadn't been so forthright with Milly, but she'd learned how to be evasive as well as how to clean by the time she came to Milly.

Nobody could fault Red's work. If she hadn't been so dark, you could think she must have Dutch blood, the way she was willing to clean outside as well as in. And though her clothes came out of the thrift shop, she kept them clean. Henrietta let Red do her own laundry while she cleaned.

"She was boiling her clothes on her old wood stove," Henrietta had said. " 'Surest way to scald yourself to death,' I told her. 'You just bring your things over here. Our well's got five gallons a minute.' "

Though Henrietta and Hart had started out as summer and weekend people just as Millie and her husband had, Hart was the sort of man who wouldn't buy a place without a good supply of water, without good insulation. Milly's house had never been intended for winter living. She had to keep the drapes pulled over her single-pane windows looking east over the channel to the mountains on the mainland, and the wind played tag with itself all over the house, which had more cracks than nails in it. It cost a fortune to heat. In summer, when the water table was low, she didn't flush the toilet more than once a day unless she had company coming. Talk about being put out to pasture!

The sudden roar of the vacuum cleaner reminded Milly that she should be dressed and out of the bedroom before Red wanted to clean it. Milly hated the sound of that machine. It reminded her of her mother, who had used it as a weapon to get Milly out of bed on a weekend morning. All her life she had hated to go to bed and hated to get up in the morning. Here on the island, people with not a thing to do behaved as if they had a herd of cows waiting for them. Unless there was a fire, people called nine o'clock island midnight and went off home. Even

Henrietta, though she didn't go to bed early, liked her time to read. At least she didn't mind being phoned anytime before midnight if the silence of Milly's house got too much for her.

Milly stood by her closet, trying to decide what to wear. She usually put out her things the night before, but it had been five in the morning before she'd got home. She chose a plaid wool skirt, a dark blue blouse and a red sweater. Unlike most of the women who had retired to the island, Milly hadn't exchanged her city clothes for men's trousers and sweat shirts. The only concession she had made was her choice of shoes, not boots of course, but her shoes were sensible.

As she finished dressing, the phone rang. She had to close the door before she answered it to shut out the noise of the vacuum cleaner.

"I hope it's not too early," Henrietta said.

"Red woke me an hour ago," Milly said.

"Of course, it's Wednesday," Henrietta said. "I haven't managed to get myself to bed yet. I'm just home from Sadie's. I waited until her sister came on the morning boat. She needed someone with her."

"How is she?" Milly asked.

"She's not a woman with many resources," Henrietta said. "Dickie was her life."

"Why do these things have to happen?" Milly wailed.

"I always try to think the young are spared, but it isn't easy. Sadie isn't going to be able to manage anything about the funeral. I suggested we might have it here, and I wondered if you would call people about the food."

"Of course," Milly said.

There was nothing Milly enjoyed more than an excuse to tie up her party line. It suited the other parties as well who seemed to have more interest in listening to Milly's conversations than in making any of their own. Sometimes that windy open sound of someone else listening annoyed her, but more often she felt obligated to live up to their attention.

Her daughter Bonnie had said to her one night, "Mother, have you forgotten who you're talking to?"

"Well, I've nearly forgotten what you look like," Milly snapped back, her attention newly and unkindly focused.

Her "late" husband shelled out plane tickets home to their children only after extracting promises that they wouldn't also visit their mother on his money.

"Can I get into the bedroom now, Mrs. Forbes?" Red called.

"Do you have a mother?" Milly demanded as she wrenched open her bedroom door.

"Only way I know to get into a fix like this," Red said.

"Has there ever been such a thing as a grateful child?"

"Were you?" Red asked quietly.

"Me? Of course I was."

"There you are then," Red said, disappearing into the bedroom.

After speaking to Milly, Henrietta Hawkins deliberated for a moment before reaching down to unplug her phone. When Hart was still at home, she routinely had done it to protect his rest, but, since

15

he'd had to be moved into extended care on the mainland, she'd rarely indulged in that protection for herself. She had always thought, "But what if he needs me?" It was by now a futile hope. Hart no longer recognized her except as the woman who brought him ice cream. The only phone call concerning him now would be a hospital official to tell her he was dead. The dead could wait.

Henrietta had to sleep now, or at least rest, if she was to get over to see Hart tomorrow and also make arrangements to have Dickie's funeral here on Friday. She would have to leave in the morning before Red arrived.

She put a pad of paper on the night table by her side of the bed so that she could scribble down the jumble of details she would otherwise worry about forgetting. Red ought to polish Hart's grandmother's tea service, a silly thing to hang onto in this day and age when it was only appropriate for weddings and funerals, but Henrietta couldn't, when they had decided to retire here, give it up, orphan it without knowing what might become of it. Hart Jr. would simply be more lumbered with it than she was. Things!

Henrietta reached for the pad and wrote, "*Red* 1. Polish the tea service."

Writing the name made her for the first time since the fire actually think of Red and wonder what her own private grief in this matter of Dickie might be. Where had she heard Red's and Dickie's names paired recently? Certainly not from Red. That information had surprised Henrietta. Red had shown so little interest in any companions her own age that

16

Henrietta had once asked her if she wasn't lonely, so much by herself there in that little cabin.

"Sometimes," Red had said, "but the only kind of company I could get along with I'd have to make up."

Henrietta understood that. Though she often even physically ached for Hart's presence, she wanted no distracting substitutes, which even he himself would be now, getting in the way of her memory of who he had been before his strokes.

Then why had Red suddenly exchanged her solitude for the likes of Dickie John? Was it simply a succumbing to her own biology? Henrietta didn't know how old Red was, but, when she had first arrived on their doorstep, Hart had said, "That child can't be more than fourteen!"

Henrietta had struggled with her conscience about Red, wondering what parents or parent might be anguished about her. But once she'd been with them a few weeks, learning the most basic skills with such a hunger for survival, Henrietta had decided that whoever that parent had been had grossly neglected if not actually abused Red. If Henrietta could teach her to look out for herself, that was probably the best thing for Red.

But now, as Henrietta thought about Red and Dickie, she was aware of how little she had ever talked with Red about . . . life. Red had certainly never invited discussion. All the questions she asked were practical ones. Henrietta had let herself assume that Red knew more than she needed to about the seamier side of experience. Dickie was, in Henrietta's view, seamy. Poor, poor Dickie.

Why did so many beautiful children simply coarsen into adulthood? Was it in their genes? Would Red now, her childhood fallen away from her, harden into cynicism?

Henrietta hadn't had a daughter, and part of her pleasure in Red was finally being able to hand on those womanly skills that stay invisible to most men even when they're done before their eyes. But teaching her to clean and cook and take care of things didn't go far enough in teaching her how to take care of herself, to have pride of heart, to be hopeful. The young had a right to be hopeful.

Henrietta turned over and fixed her eyes on the great cedar tree which had grown by now too close to the house so that on a windy night it banged on the bedroom window as if demanding to be let inside. Hart would have had it cut down, and she would have accepted his decision as part of his need to keep her from harm though she knew harm had to come in any case.

Whoever it was up there who measured the lengths of lives had one blind eye and was all thumbs. No depth perception, none at all.

Chapter II

A brisk southeasterly was blowing as Karen
Tasuki parked her car near the ferry toll booth. She
was early as she liked to be. There was time to be
patient with her cold hands unlocking the door,
leisurely in arranging the cash drawer and tickets. It
was still dark, and her first customer approached in a
blaze of headlights.

"One thing I'll say for you," said Riley, one of
her firefighting companions. "You're here."

Even such parsimonious praise was encouraging.
For the younger, unmarried men, working for the

ferries was too tame a job, but even so they were reluctant to see a woman doing it.

"Thanks," Karen said, handing him his ticket and change. "Lane one . . ."

"Don't tell me to have a good day," Riley said. "It's going to be a bitch."

He drove off to park in lane one before Karen could ask him why or express sympathy. She was used now to these off-hand personal remarks, tossed like empty beer cans out of car windows by young men who seemed to think of any reply as in the nature of a fine. Their lack of ordinary civility often annoyed Karen, but this morning the young men of the island were made of very vulnerable flesh, and she felt protective, concerned.

The next car was the island's only taxi, driven by a pale, hardly awake young man. The ancient Miss James was in the back seat, holding out her three dollars for a foot passenger ticket.

"You don't need to pay this morning, Miss James," Karen shouted. "It's Thursday."

"I forgot," the driver shouted in his turn. "You're a senior. You don't have to pay on weekdays."

"Of course not," Miss James said, impatient with herself as she stuffed her money back into her wallet.

The cab moved down onto the dock to deliver Miss James to the waiting room, built on the east side of the dock just short of the loading ramp, welcome shelter on a windy morning like this one.

The first light of dawn came like a bucket of dirty water thrown across the southeast edge of the sky.

Henrietta Hawkins was next in line. She, too, was over sixty-five, but Karen had to collect twelve dollars for her car.

20

"This car's old enough to travel free on weekdays," Henrietta said as she handed over the bills.

It was a joking protest she often made, but she never complained frankly of the cost of traveling back and forth a couple of times a week to see a husband who no longer recognized her. She always looked cheerful, partly because she always wore a series of brightly colored scarves which lit her face and set off her handsome head of white hair. Karen wished she could make some acknowledging comment, like sending her regards to Mr. Hawkins, but he had been taken off the island a couple of years before she had arrived.

"Karen," Henrietta said, as she accepted her ticket, "the funeral for Dickie is going to be at my house tomorrow. Red will be there getting it ready today, and Milly's organizing the food. I was wondering if you could speak to a few of the young men and find out if one of them wants to give a eulogy, or maybe several of them would just like to say a few words. There isn't to be a service, prayers or anything of that sort. Sadie said Dickie hated that sort of thing."

"I'll ask them," Karen said. "I'm working at the pub tonight. Riley's on this sailing."

"Good. I'll speak to him myself. It's going to be at noon; so the men can come on their lunch break."

"Oh," Karen said as Henrietta's car started forward, "Miss James is going in this morning."

"Fine. I'll take her. She's probably going to her dentist. It's on my way."

The bus service into Vancouver, once adequate, was now intolerable. It had taken Karen some months

21

to learn which drivers of cars going onto the ferry were comfortably willing to accommodate foot passengers. There were some drivers — Dickie had been among them — who made a point of driving so recklessly that they wouldn't ever be inconvenienced. But young men like Rat and Adam were surprisingly amiable about it, even if they were taken out of their way. Riley was reliably unreliable. This morning nobody would be safe with him.

Karen couldn't have believed in summer when she had first been hired that she'd ever like this job, the huge lines of tourist traffic, people too late to pick up their car reservations, whole families of tired kids and frustrated parents left behind with nobody but Karen to blame and nowhere to spend the night. She hadn't known the islanders from the tourists, which ferocious dogs in the backs of pickup trucks were just bluffing, which might lunge for a patch of uniform and flesh. The troubles of winter — getting up in the dark, the wind blowing, ferries often delayed by rough seas, sometimes even cancelled — were experiences she shared with people she now knew.

After selling the final several tickets, Karen took her keys to unlock the ramp controls and walked down the short line of cars, smiling. She signaled Riley, first in line, onto the dock and then followed him. The wind was fresh and the heavy sky was now washed with modest pinks.

In the pass the ferry sounded, and the sea gulls parading on the dock railings rose up in noisy anticipation, for some of them would also choose to ride the ferry across the strait. The pigeons paced and racketed about the ramp, full of fretful cooing.

Out on the lightening water rode several varieties of ducks.

Lights were now on in most of the houses around the bay, and smoke from their chimneys made a layer of grey underneath the layer of cloud. Karen wondered when she had learned to distinguish between island mists and smoke.

The ferry, brightly lighted, came round the point promptly at eight o'clock. Karen knew that everyone waiting to go aboard would take its being on time as a good omen for their day. She herself felt competent lowering the large ramp onto the ferry deck, raising the barrier, and greeting the ferry hand who came to collect her data. There were no foot passengers coming off and from the adjacent island only a couple of work trucks which would be lined up tonight to go home. Once they disembarked, Karen waved the several departing foot passengers aboard, among them the ancient Miss James who was tall and thin and erect, in a proper town hat and good winter coat.

"Mrs. Hawkins is going to give you a lift into town," Karen shouted.

"Thank you, child," Miss James replied. She called everyone under forty "child," everyone over forty "my good man" or "my good woman," her solution to her failing memory for names.

When the passengers had crossed the car deck to the stairs that would lead them up into the lounges, Karen switched the light to green and waved the cars aboard, one last time wishing her travelers well.

The only difficulty about a prompt ferry was that it meant Karen had to kill a little time before she could have morning coffee at the store and then pick up her mail. There was a kettle in the booth, but coffee was an excuse to be with people. When she had first taken the job with its odd hours, she thought what a virtue it would be to have most mornings to herself, but, if she didn't have a specific chore, the laundry or the cleaning, she hated going back to her beach cottage and its silence. She didn't even like to watch the birds, as she did when she was out here on the dock with so much else to do.

Walking back down the dock, Karen wondered if she would ever get used to being alone. She had lived with Peggy for eight years. Would it take her eight more years to get over it? And if she did get over it, would she be so set in her ways that she could never live with anyone else again?

If Peggy could see her on a morning like this or in the pub at night, she wouldn't recognize her. For Karen had never had a job in those eight years. Peggy had wanted her to be at home. "I want to be entirely looked after," Peggy had said. Eventually, for reasons Karen still didn't really understand, Peggy had felt she was doing the looking after because she paid all the bills. When Karen finally asked, "What is really wrong?" Peggy had answered bluntly, "You're boring." It was that accusation Karen couldn't face in her empty house, for surely that about her hadn't changed, however busy she had kept herself. In her blank misery, she bored herself.

Often Henrietta stayed in her car for the fifty-minute ride across the strait, sparing herself the long climb up the stairs and the negative social demands of people who wanted to kill time in chatter. How few people could simply watch the sea for a breaking killer whale, the sky for an eagle, the horizon for weather shaping over the mountains. How few people could simply think or read a book. This morning, however, she had to speak to Riley and then find Miss James to offer her a ride.

She found Riley in the cafeteria, head bowed over a large plate of greasy eggs, bacon, and chips. He had not bothered to shave or comb his hair, and he might as well have had a sign hanging around his neck saying Do Not Disturb.

"I'm sorry to interrupt your breakfast, Riley," Henrietta said, taking a seat across from him.

He looked at her and sighed.

"It won't take long," Henrietta reassured him. "I wondered if you had anything you'd like to say at Dickie's funeral tomorrow."

"Me?" Riley asked, incredulous.

"It's very hard on a community to lose someone as young as Dickie."

"I should think most of you old people would be glad to see the last of him," Riley said with sullen anger.

"Riley, most of us have known Dickie all his life, saw him lose his father, saw him drop out of school and then gradually pull himself together, building himself that house, getting himself the truck and working hard for it all. He was still a boy to most of us, still figuring out how to live."

Again Riley sighed, but Henrietta could read an opening vulnerability in his dark eyes.

"You were his friend," she coaxed.

"I bought him his last drink," Riley said softly.

"Oh, Riley, I'm sorry," Henrietta said, and she put a hand on his arm.

After a moment, Riley said, "Yeah, well, I guess maybe I could do something. I'm sort of torn up about it, you know?"

"Of course you are," Henrietta said, and she stood up. "It will be at noon at my house."

"Good excuse for a shave," he said, a hand on his stubbly cheek, and he gave her a rueful grin.

So many people these days, without a church to offer some structure for grief, wanted to let the dead go without public acknowledgement. But one of the points of a funeral was to make people take that first step, begin to pull themselves together. Riley would be the better for a shave and he knew it. And, once they were all gathered together, it would be easier for them to realize that, if they felt any responsibility for Dickie's death, they all shared it, and it became a more honest weight, one with a meaning for the future. She knew. She had buried a son of her own.

Miss James was sitting alone in the lounge, looking out at the somber morning. When Henrietta put a hand on her shoulder, she started.

"Sorry," Henrietta said.

"I was riding the ferry from Oakland to San Francisco before the Bay Bridge was built," Miss James confessed.

"You still may want a lift into Vancouver," Henrietta said loudly.

"Thanks, Hen," Miss James said. "That woman called me about the funeral."

"Oh, I hope you don't think you have to bring anything."

"Of course I do. I'm past baking, but I can bring a pound of coffee."

"Worth its weight in gold," Henrietta said apologetically.

"Well, money's to spend. Everyone who might have been waiting for me to die is dead themselves, long since."

"Where are you going today?"

Miss James frowned at her.

Henrietta repeated her question.

"To my ear man," Miss James answered wryly. "I'm going to ask him if an ear trumpet wouldn't do better than this gadget."

"I'll see you at the car then," Henrietta said and moved on.

Miss James was the only person on the island who was never called anything but Miss James. Only a few people, Henrietta among them, knew that she had been christened Lily Anne, which probably hadn't had such a silly ring at the turn of the century in the South where Miss James had been born. There was hardly a trace of it in her voice, except when she pronounced names like Mary or Arthur. In Mary the "r" was pronounced and stretched. In Arthur, there was no "r" at all. It was a nomadic accent with traces of many dialects, its only true country great old age, a flat and windy plain. Miss James wouldn't thank Henrietta for the stab of pity she felt at that deaf isolation.

In the car Miss James chose, as most deaf people do, to talk since she could not listen, but she was attentive enough to fall silent at the moments when the traffic piled up or Henrietta had a difficult turn to negotiate. Miss James was for Henrietta an ideal passenger.

"There's something I'd like you to think about, Hen," Miss James said as they were delivered from the Massey tunnel. "I want to do something for Red. I've been thinking about it for some time. She's too young to have nobody in the world. Oh, she might marry, I suppose, but I wouldn't like to see her marry for that reason. She *can* live alone. I was thinking of leaving her my house. It isn't much of a place, but at least it's got electricity and indoor plumbing, and I think it would suit her. But sometimes I'm afraid I'm going to live forever. When I think of that child dead in his bed . . ."

For a moment Henrietta didn't realize Miss James was referring to Dickie, but there was no distance between child and boy in Miss James' long view.

"If I knew I'd be dead in a year, that would suit me for her, but longer seems too long. I thought of telling her, but she might feel obligated, and I don't want that."

"Why not?" asked Henrietta, for whom obligation had been a kind guide. But Miss James didn't hear the question.

"I give her a bonus at Christmas," Miss James continued, "but that's only fair. And to tell the truth, I don't think she spends the money she earns. She has no rent to speak of. She collects her own wood, grows her own vegetables. She doesn't run a car. She hasn't even got a phone. And she certainly doesn't spend it on clothes. I don't suppose she knows what a bank account is. It wouldn't surprise me if she kept her money in a sock under her mattress or buried it in a jar in her garden."

Henrietta made a mental note to ask Red what she did do with her money. It had never occurred to her to teach Red about banking, but of course she should have.

"But she'd know what to do with a house. She takes care of it now as if it were her own," Miss James concluded.

For the first time it struck Henrietta that there could be a pleasure in being childless, that someone with even Miss James' limited resources was free to speculate on generosity, to bestow it where she chose, unlike Henrietta who considered herself in stewardship over what would be Hart Jr.'s and then his children's legacy. It would never have occurred to Henrietta to give Red anything but her attention.

"We'll talk about it," Henrietta shouted just before she let Miss James out of the car.

Then Henrietta pulled up beside The Big Scoop to get Hart his pint of peppermint ice cream.

Milly admired and resented the way Henrietta could delegate authority and then simply take off for a day in town, leaving a dozen or so women to do all the work for a funeral she'd take credit for. Well, be given credit for anyway. Milly had never baked anything that wasn't ready-mixed, and usually she went to a bakery until she had moved to the island where, though nobody said anything, you were expected to turn up at every bake sale with something made from scratch — an apt expression that, for Milly's own disastrous first attempts.

"Get a specialty," Henrietta had advised her. A

solution which, Milly knew, would only add boredom to frustration.

Milly had taken a page out of Hen's book and delegated all the baking and even the sandwich-making. But still twenty years away from her old age pension, she couldn't get away with a box of tea bags for her own contribution. She could manage making radishes into little flowers, carrots and celery into little fans, and arrange a tolerably good-looking and appetizing tray with dip in the middle (though she never served dip at her own house out of fear for her carpet), and some olives scattered around.

Her idea of a party was getting dressed up and going out either empty-handed or occasionally with a bottle of wine or a box of mints to a meal someone else prepared, served, and cleaned up after. People didn't give parties like that on this island. You took potluck, which was just that, given all the young vegetarians on the island. And afterwards, you did the dishes; they were part of the fun. Henrietta was one of the few people on the island with enough water for a dishwasher, but she didn't have one.

"The simple life," Forbes had called it when he bought this place fifteen years ago.

Had it been in the back of his mind even then that it would be a place to park her? This whole island was a large used-wife lot, more widows than divorcees, but even the women with their men still around were *used*.

"If you had your choice, you wouldn't go back to the city, would you?" Henrietta had asked her.

"In a minute!" Milly had answered.

"You want to live in the city?" Forbes had

taunted her. "Go work for it then, the way everyone else does."

All very well for him to say, but what could Milly do? She'd have to work in a stationer's shop or a ladies' dress shop and not make enough to rent anything but someone's basement suite.

"So consider yourself fortunate," he had said.

How did men get away with it? There Forbes had stood, promising "Until death do us part" before God and everybody they knew, and he could still say to her, twenty years down the road, "I have other plans for the rest of my life." And apparently there wasn't a thing she could do about it. A man could go to jail for stealing her purse; yet Forbes went scot free after stealing twenty years of her life, leaving her years she could not now give away.

Not that Milly wanted to marry again. Who would be fool enough to fall for that twice? "Wash your own socks," she snarled at her imagined suitor.

There was a second timid knock before Milly realized there was someone at her kitchen door. Nobody on the island used a front door. Jane, Homer's wife, stood with a baking pan in her hand.

"I'm sorry to bother you," she said, "but I can't go tomorrow. I promised my daughter I'd go over for the day and stay with the baby while she goes to the dentist."

"Come in," Milly said.

"Oh, isn't that pretty?" Jane exclaimed at the tray of raw vegetables. "It looks like something in a fancy restaurant."

Milly shrugged. She could still remember the first night Forbes had complimented her on the dinner instead of on her own good looks.

31

"Homer's going, but I didn't like to ask him to take this," Jane said, nodding at the pan. "You know what men are like, remembering."

"Some of them even forget their wives," Milly said wryly.

"Poor Hen," Jane said. "I don't think I could take it."

It was Forbes Milly had in mind, but it wasn't a new experience for her to see the sympathy she bid for won by someone else. It was very like the way she played bridge.

"Cup of coffee?" Milly suggested.

"I shouldn't, but . . ."

They sat at the kitchen table, a habit Milly had given in to because her living room in winter was so dark and gloomy, but it still gave her an odd feeling, as if she were a servant entertaining behind the back of the lady of the house.

"These are such pretty cups," Jane said, her gardener's hands uncertain and careful.

They had been wedding presents, and Milly had once thought them pretty, too. But they mocked her now, as did Jane's envy of them. Jane didn't need cups; she had a husband, even if he was just poor old weather-beaten Homer.

"Did you ever want to leave the island?" Milly asked.

"When I was young," Jane answered. "I had all sorts of fancy notions about going to England to study to be a nurse or a midwife, but my dad said I could learn as much helping with the lambing. Anyway, there wasn't the money. I probably only thought I wanted to. I wasn't used to strangers. So many of them do leave now, and I guess that's best if you think about what happened to Dickie."

"It could have happened anywhere," Milly said.

"Sadie said it was because of that girl," Jane ventured.

"Red? Who'd break his heart for Red?" Milly asked.

"You break your heart for whoever's there," Jane said.

"Oh, I don't know, Jane," Milly said. "Did Dickie have a heart? Do any of them?"

"He wasn't that bad," Jane protested, and she burst into tears.

Milly cried with her from that vast store of menopausal tears which could be squandered.

"Well," Jane said, recovering. "I guess I needed that. I couldn't break down in front of Sadie."

Milly blotted her eyes carefully.

"Homer's dinner!" Jane said suddenly and got up.

"Homer's dinner," Milly repeated when Jane had gone, and she cut a large square from the pan of brownies Jane had left behind.

Servant no longer, Milly was now a naughty child in her own kitchen. She cut another square and poured herself another cup of coffee. Before she was through, she had eaten half the pan.

Who's to know, she thought. She could take the rest out and put them on a plate.

Chapter III

"People usually get on with the eating and drinking after the body's decently buried," Milly said as she helped Henrietta unfold the large linen cloth to cover the extended dining room table.

"Sadie wouldn't hear of it," Henrietta said. "If it's a party for Dickie, he has to be here."

"Where are you going to put him?" Milly asked, looking around the large but amply furnished living room.

"In Hart's den," Henrietta said. "That way, a few people at a time . . ."

"Is Sadie going to sit in there with him?" Milly asked.

"I doubt it. She'll do what she can, poor soul."

Henrietta lifted the shining tea service from the sideboard, put it on the table and stood back to admire it. Milly began to take the cups from their hooks in the glass-fronted china cupboard.

"Don't you fear for these?" Milly asked as she set them out.

"I'd be grateful to anyone who broke one," Henrietta admitted. "There is so much too much of it."

"I suppose, if you didn't have it, you wouldn't get yourself into things like this," Milly speculated sympathetically. "There's always the hall or the school gym."

There was a knock at the front door. The two women exchanged surprised glances.

"It must be the undertaker," Henrietta decided, checking her watch to see if the ferry from Vancouver Island could have arrived.

The two men at the door seemed almost indecently young for their job, and for a moment Henrietta thought they might be Jehovah's Witnesses. Then she caught sight of the hearse in the drive.

"If you'll just bring it . . . him in here," she said, showing them the den.

"Shall we, like, move that couch?" one of them asked.

"Oh, could you?" Henrietta said.

The furniture rearranged, they went out for the coffin, distressingly ornate, winking with brass, and placed it on the floor where the couch had been.

"You want us back here at two."

"Yes," Henrietta said.

When she'd let them out, she turned back to Milly.

"Well," Milly said, "the guest of honor has arrived."

"I picked some winter-flowering jasmine this morning, and I bought yellow roses in town yesterday."

"I'll do the roses if you like," Milly offered. "It's one of the few things I'm good at. I told Forbes before we were married that I was a girl who had to be sent roses."

"And did he?"

"Still does, on the anniversary of our divorce, the bastard!"

The two sprays of jasmine sat on the floor at each end of the coffin, and Milly stood with the bowl of roses.

"On the coffin, I think," Henrietta decided.

"No peeking, right?" Milly asked as she set them down.

"Who would be tempted?"

"Now," Milly said, stepping back, "that looks cheerful."

"I think I've decided against candles," Henrietta said.

"Too much like church," Milly agreed.

At eleven-thirty the women began to arrive with the food. Several of the younger ones came in first with babies who were deposited in their baskets on Henrietta's bed. Then the young mothers went back out for their food. The table wasn't large enough for it all. Pans of fried chicken, bowls of salad, plates of smoked salmon, loaves of homemade bread, cookies, pies, and cakes filled all the kitchen counters, and two huge pots of clam chowder were put on the stove.

"Bowls," Henrietta said.

"We brought them from the hall."

"You do think of everything!" Henrietta exclaimed.

"Who's bringing Sadie?"

"Jane probably."

"Jane's in town," Milly said. "Homer said he'd pick her up."

"Hey!" Rat's wife suddenly said. "Where's the body?"

"In the den," Henrietta replied.

"Is that where Sadie's going to be?"

The women moved timidly to see the coffin for themselves and admire the flowers.

"Would one of you light the fire in there?" Henrietta called over the heads of her guests.

"Do you think we should? Would it remind her?"

"The coffin will remind her."

Henrietta left them to debate the question and come to their own conclusion. If you couldn't look on what killed, you'd go blind.

Miss James presented herself at the back door. "The cab was late; so the coffee is late," she said as she eyed the large electric pot, its red light indicating that the coffee was already made.

"Never mind," Henrietta shouted. "We'll probably have to make another."

"Now don't try to make me comfortable," Miss James said as she took off her coat. "I'm no good at crowds. I'll just sit where Sadie can see I'm here."

At that moment Sadie John appeared, dressed in black, leaning heavily on Homer's arm.

"She could use a bit of coffee," Homer said to Henrietta.

"I could use," Sadie said slowly and carefully, "a bit of gin."

"Later, Sadie, I promise," Henrietta said. "Have some coffee now. I'll just take your coat."

That task was accomplished with some little difficulty, but finally Henrietta could hand on an armload of coats to be put in the guest room. She and Homer led Sadie to a chair in the living room and had her settled with a cup of coffee before the men began to arrive.

"Where have you put him?" Sadie asked.

"In the den," Henrietta explained.

"I don't want to go in there."

"You don't have to."

"I don't want to look at the coffin. I told them, make it nice."

"They have. You don't have to."

The men brought a new weight into the gathering. Most of them wore ties. The shopkeepers were in dark suits. Their wives directed them, a few at a time, into the den, but they didn't have to be encouraged to pay their respects to Sadie, even if all they could think to say was, "Buck up now, old girl!" or "That is a fine coffin!"

It was the young men, Henrietta was pleased to notice, who took time with Sadie, sitting down beside her. Riley, who had not only shaved but put on a jacket and tie, had even persuaded her to have a sandwich.

38

Karen Tasuki arrived late and out of breath. "I thought the eleven-ten from Swartz Bay would never come in. Has Rat spoken to you?"

"No," Henrietta said.

"They're going to wait until just before it's time to go to the graveyard and then, sort of, propose toasts. That way they thought anyone could join in who wanted to, and nobody would have to make a real speech."

As she spoke, Karen unwrapped the plate she had brought.

Milly, refilling the silver coffee pot, looked over and said, "What on earth is that?"

"Sushi," Karen said defensively.

"It's great stuff," young Adam said, taking a piece of the seaweed-bound delicacy and saving Henrietta from having to make that gesture herself with less genuine enthusiasm.

"Foreign," Milly said.

"My great-grandfather is buried in this graveyard," Karen suddenly announced. "People have been eating sushi here for generations."

"That grave's your great-grandfather's, no kidding?" Adam asked.

But Karen had put the plate down and left the kitchen.

"How could that be?" Milly demanded.

"A lot of this island was owned by Japanese before they were rounded up and sent to the Kootenays during the war," Homer said.

"You wonder why she'd want to come back," Milly said, "why she'd want to admit it."

"Well, it's nothing to be ashamed of after all,

Milly," Henrietta said more sharply than she'd intended, but really sometimes Milly behaved as if she didn't have good sense.

"We're the ones who should be ashamed," Homer said quietly, but he helped himself to a leg of fried chicken.

The food was being eaten solemnly but steadily in all the crowded rooms, even in the den where Dickie's charred bones lay under their light burden of roses. The talk in that room was about Dickie. Even an occasional remark was addressed to him. And the fire burned cheerfully.

Finally Rat said to Henrietta, "Do you think it's about time?"

She looked at the clock on the mantel. It was one-thirty.

"Yes, Rat, if you please."

Rat took a spoon and tapped a glass until the crowd in the living room fell silent except for those shushing the people in the den and kitchen.

Adam, who had been sitting next to Sadie, got to his feet. He shifted shoulders too broad for the suit jacket he was wearing.

"Hen thought we ought to take a few minutes now for anybody to say anything they'd like to. I'm no good at making speeches so I just want to say that Dickie was my best friend, maybe because he was my worst competition with women and darts. I'm going to miss him. Life may be easier, but it's going to be a lot less fun."

One by one the young men took their turns, and Henrietta was glad to be reminded that Dickie was a man other men had genuinely liked. Though Sadie was now weeping, surely to hear her son spoken of so warmly would give her some comfort.

Riley was the last of them to speak. Smaller-bodied, slighter than Adam, he spoke with more natural confidence and he ended his remarks by thanking Henrietta for giving them the opportunity to say good-bye to Dickie, everyone together.

The room had fallen silent as Henrietta opened the front door to the undertakers. Rat and Adam and Riley moved to help them lift the coffin. As they carried it back through the living room, Miss James in her flat, loud voice began to recite:

> The time you won your town the race
> We chaired you through the market-place;
> Man and boy stood cheering by,
> And home we brought you shoulder-high
>
> Today, the road all runners come,
> Shoulder high we bring you home,
> And set you at your threshold down,
> Townsman of a stiller town.

The coffin was gone from the room and in the hearse before Miss James spoke the final lines:

> And round that early-laurelled head
> Will flock to gaze the strengthless dead
> And find unwithered on its curls
> The garland briefer than a girl's.

Then Sadie cried out, "I can't go. I just can't!"

"You don't have to, dear," Henrietta said to her,

an arm around her shoulder. "You can stay right here and have that gin."

"Can I catch a ride with you?" Rat asked Karen. "My wife's going to stay to help clean up and then take the baby home."

"Sure," Karen said.

"Where do you suppose Red was?" Rat asked as they waited in Karen's car to take their place in line behind the hearse.

"I don't know," Karen said.

"Miss James was something, wasn't she? I'm sure glad at least one woman said something."

"I didn't know him at all well," Karen said defensively.

"I guess the ones who did wouldn't have had much to say about him either, but he just hadn't settled down yet, that's all."

"I thought you all did a really good job," Karen said.

"Yeah, well, Dickie was a good buddy. Anybody'd have to say that about him. But it makes you think, doesn't it, about how much anybody could say about any of us?"

Karen wanted to protest, but she herself couldn't have counted on anyone to stand up and say anything about her. It wasn't simply that she was new to this community; she'd forgotten how to make friends. She'd left none behind her in the city. All the people she had known were Peggy's friends.

She swung her car into line behind Homer's, turning on her lights at his example. They drove at about fifteen miles an hour over the narrow, twisting island road. In the grey day the only brightness was a patch of shallow snow here and there under the trees where the rain hadn't reached to melt it. They drove right by Dickie's turnoff, but neither she nor Rat glanced up through the trees to see where the chimney still stood.

Though there were no more than a dozen cars, there wasn't room for them all to park in the roundabout at the gate of the graveyard. They parked on the upper road and walked down, just a small band now. Karen was the only woman, but she and the men were accustomed to that. Not only at fire practice but often near closing time at the pub she was alone with them.

They all stood quietly while the undertakers lowered the coffin by means of pulleys into the freshly dug grave, the mourners' interest in the mechanism distracting them from what it was achieving. High above in the branches of a huge dead tree, a bald eagle observed them, and out in the pass sea lions sported and barked. In the grass at their feet, a few snowdrops bloomed.

When the coffin was in place, the men took turns shoveling in the dirt. Karen stood a little apart, and no one offered her a turn. She didn't care. She was here only because she couldn't have borne to stay behind at the house with all the women, with that awful Milly Forbes.

Why, Karen wondered, had she said that about her great-grandfather? She had no idea where he was buried — one of the Gulf Islands was all her father had ever said, aside from telling her not to be an ancestor worshiper. She was to be one hundred and

43

fifty percent Canadian the way he pretended to be. She at least had the advantage of her mother's blue eyes.

But she had often walked down here and looked at that Japanese grave, and, though she couldn't read the characters, it had given her some sense of her roots. If it wasn't likely to be the grave of her great-grandfather, it could have been. Only claiming it like that had turned into a lie. She'd never look at the grave again without burning embarrassment. She kept her back to it now.

I'll never belong here, she thought, *or anywhere.* And bleak as the thought was, it had an odd comfort in it, perhaps because it was the truth.

"I'd better take Sadie home while she can still walk," Milly said to Henrietta.

Milly wanted the excuse to leave. Cleaning up after a party always depressed her, and this one had already ruined her eye make-up.

"Hen's a kind woman," Sadie said as she sat slumped in Milly's car, holding the bowl of roses in her lap, never having seen them on the coffin. "A kind, kind woman."

If a little smug and self-righteous, Milly thought. Milly had no such aspirations, and therefore she didn't envy her friend Hen's hard-earned place in this community. As for herself, she didn't intend to live by the side of the road and be a friend to man. Henrietta could talk all she liked, but Milly hadn't seen her eat any of those revolting little raw fish and seaweed balls. What a thing to bring! They *were* white people, after all. What was that girl trying to prove? Her great-grandfather buried in the graveyard indeed!

"I feel bad," Sadie said.

"Well, of course you do," Milly said, trying to keep her irritation out of her voice.

"I mean sick," Sadie moaned, and she threw up into the roses.

"Oh Sadie!"

"It was the smell of them," Sadie mumbled.

Milly frantically wound down her window before she herself gagged on the awful mixture of odors which now filled the car. It was all she could do not to slam on the brakes and order this disgusting creature out of the car.

"I'm just worn out," Sadie said and sighed.

Milly drove at dangerous speeds to keep the fresh air coming in as well as to get this over as quickly as possible. Finally she pulled up on the road outside Sadie's rundown little cottage and waited for her to get out of the car.

"I'm just worn out," Sadie said again, staring out the window.

Now that the car had stopped, the smell was overpowering.

"You're home, Sadie," Milly said sharply.

"I know," Sadie said vaguely. "It's not like I saw much of him, but at least I knew he was there."

Was she unaware that she was sitting in her own stinking vomit? Milly flung open her own door and got out. For a moment, she simply stood, breathing. Then she went around to Sadie's door and opened it.

"Come on. You need to get yourself cleaned up, and then you can rest."

"Built himself a house and moved out is what he did. Now there's not even that."

"Sadie, come on!"

"What's the point of them?" Sadie asked sadly. "What's the point of them, can you tell me that?"

"Get out of this car, Sadie, right now!" Milly demanded, taking the roses from her and flinging them, bowl and all, into the ditch. If Hen had been telling the truth, she'd thank Milly for one less bowl.

"It was the smell of them," Sadie said again.

Finally she struggled out of the car and staggered up her path while Milly stood watching her. Once Sadie managed to make it up her rickety steps and through the door, Milly wound down the passenger window, too, and drove home in freezing wind.

At her own house, she filled a bucket with hot soapy water and sloshed out the floor of her car.

Then she went to the phone and dialed. "Hen, you won't believe this, but that woman vomited all over my car and broke your lovely bowl!"

Chapter IV

"It's a funny thing," Henrietta said to Red as they sat together eating leftover clam chowder for their lunch, "all that time I was trying to teach you how to live alone and really take care of yourself, I was teaching myself, too. Do you make sure you have at least one hot meal a day?"

"Mostly."

"I do only because I told you to," Henrietta confessed. "Even so, I often have to invite someone else over to make myself cook."

"Miss James says it's easier to live alone if you always have," Red said.

"I suppose it is. She's very fond of you, you know."

Red didn't respond.

"Red, you need to know people care about you. It's nothing to be embarrassed about. This is your community."

Red looked at her skeptically.

"Why didn't you come to the funeral?"

"You had enough help, didn't you?" Red asked.

"Oh, help, yes, but that isn't what I meant."

"Sadie's telling everyone it was my fault."

"Where did you hear that?" Henrietta asked.

Red shrugged.

"Sadie's naturally upset," Henrietta said, "but that's nothing to take to heart."

"I don't. It doesn't matter to me what people say."

On the contrary, Henrietta thought. At any suggestion of criticism or interference Red withdrew into her own well-defended territory.

"I only thought, if you liked Dickie, it would be only natural . . ."

"I didn't like Dickie," Red replied firmly, and she got up to clear the table.

Sometimes it puzzled Henrietta that she could be so concerned for someone as bluntly uncompromising as Red when the whole art of life for Henrietta was graceful compromise. She knew she would have to let an hour or so pass before any conversation could resume.

On the days she was at home, Henrietta's habit was to rest after lunch, not an indulgence but a way

48

to store up strength for the days she had to go to the mainland. Usually she read until she was about to doze off and then got up. She had nothing against sleeping during the day except the dreams she had, embarrassing rather than really nightmarish. In them, she seemed to be drunk, unable to cross a room or navigate stairs without falling down, all the while trying to pretend nothing was wrong, and curiously no one else in those dreams ever did seem to notice either her embarrassment or her distress. They behaved, just as she was trying to behave, as if nothing were wrong.

Today her book didn't hold her attention. Her own concerns kept intruding on the plot. Sometimes Red could behave as if these last four years of their slow building of understanding simply didn't exist, as if Henrietta were just another intrusive old woman without any special status in Red's heart. It wasn't gratitude Henrietta wanted. In fact, Red even in her most taciturn moments had odd ways of showing not gratitude so much as loyalty, like her wanting to know that Henrietta hadn't really needed her at Dickie's funeral. If Henrietta had asked her to be there, Red would have come, whatever her personal feelings. No, what Henrietta wanted from Red was trust. It was exactly at those moments when Henrietta was offering her good will that Red drew back.

Was Henrietta somehow too ambitious for Red, not in a material way, not in any conventionally social way, but too ambitious for her spirit? Red wasn't afraid of work and its obligations. She was generous with her time and energy even with people she didn't particularly like. She wasn't, however, generous in giving anyone the benefit of the doubt. Didn't Red have the right to be happier than she was?

"What's happy?" she could hear Red ask, in a voice a hundred years older than any of them.

None of the young people seemed to Henrietta as happy as she had been at their age, or was she just not remembering what it had really been like?

She put her book down and got up. Red was washing the windows in the living room which looked out over the pass.

"You know, it doesn't seem to me you young people have as much fun as we used to at your age. I remember fishing trips and picnics and dances at the hall."

"You were on holiday," Red said. "There must have been people who lived and worked here even then."

"Well, of course," Henrietta said.

Most of their friends had been on holiday, too. It was only after she and Hart had come to live here that those distinctions began to blur.

"I wouldn't want to be a weekender," Red said. "I'd rather be here or not be here."

"Do you ever think about leaving the island?"

"No," Red said, "never."

"Never's a long time," Henrietta said.

"Maybe."

"If you're going to make anything of your life, you have to think that way, at your age that is."

"Well, I just don't," Red said.

"Do you save any of the money you earn, Red?"

Red glanced over her shoulder at Henrietta.

"Or is that a question you'd have to lie about?"

"Oh, I guess not," Red said, grinning, "only it would sound like I'd been lying before if I said I did."

"Not lying. Oversimplifying maybe."

"I like to keep things simple."

"Have you got a bank account?"

"No."

"Would you like me to take you into town and show you how to open one?"

"No."

"Money is safe in a bank account, and it earns interest," Henrietta urged. "You can make your money work for you."

"I don't need all that much of it," Red said and moved off to the windows in Hart's study.

On the Friday nights Karen had ferry duty, she was also supposed to turn up at the pub between the time the 6:10 p.m. boat left for the mainland and when it returned with its weekend load of passengers at 8:30. If the boat was on time, Karen could help serve dinners for almost an hour and a half. But sometimes she had less than an hour, and she worried that the pub owner might finally decide that her conflict of schedules made her less attractive an employee than several others who were in line for the job.

Tonight Adam said to her as she hurriedly served him his fish and chips, "You only just got here, didn't you?"

51

"Yes, but I'm on for the eight-thirty ferry."

"Next thing you know, you'll be driving the oil truck! How many jobs does one person need?"

Adam had a light in his eye which made it difficult for Karen to read his tone. The only male flirts she knew were gay, which Adam certainly was not. He was criticizing her.

Later, selling the few tickets to people going to other islands on the night boat, Karen wondered how much she was criticized for getting more than her share of the limited winter work. Most people her age who were not working were collecting unemployment insurance, and it was a way of life for them to work just long enough to qualify for it, live on it until it ran out, and then look for work again. Only single mothers with at least two children could go on welfare. Single people were expected to move on if they couldn't support themselves here.

Red was virtually the only other woman Karen knew who didn't pattern her life in such terms. Karen suspected that Red had a principle about it, though perhaps not the same principle as her own. Karen never wanted to be dependent again, whether on a person or on the government, whose tolerance for boring dependents was also limited.

She was already down at the ramp when the lighted ferry appeared around the point, its searchlight casting for navigational landmarks, one of which was a cottage at bayside. Karen would not have liked to live with that distinction before each winter dawn, after each winter nightfall, the fingering light finding its own reflection in her exposed windows.

She lowered the ramp. The first car off the boat,

instead of proceeding along the dock, stopped where she stood.

"Hey, Karen!"

There were Sally and Sarah, two friends of Peggy's who hadn't been paired a year ago when Karen had left Vancouver.

"You'll have to move along," Karen said, frantically gesturing.

"Sure, but we want to see you."

"Pull off up there on the road by the big map," Karen instructed.

The driver of the car behind them honked impatiently and glared at Karen as he passed. No islander would ever do that, Karen reassured herself with her now firmly in place island prejudice against tourists. No islander would stop like that with a ferry attendant either, except in an emergency. What on earth were Sally and Sarah doing on this island in the middle of winter?

Karen saw the few cars onto the ferry and walked reluctantly back up the ramp.

"Where are you staying?" she asked.

"We brought our sleeping bags. We thought maybe we could crash with you," Sally said, arching her ample eyebrows.

"I don't have much room," Karen said doubtfully, "and I have to work at the pub tonight."

"Great!" Sally said. "We can go to the pub."

"It's not really your sort of pub," Karen warned them.

"All the better. Local color," Sarah said.

So they followed Karen back to work where she settled them at a small corner table, out of the main traffic. Karen was glad it was an unusually busy evening. She didn't want to seem to ignore them, but she didn't want to encourage their familiarity with all the island watching. Fear had dried her mouth and dampened her shirt. Among the locals, Sally and Sarah called no particular attention to themselves in their jeans and hiking boots. But, if they began to behave as if they were on home turf, Karen couldn't imagine what might happen.

"Hey, what about introducing us to your friends?" Adam asked with the same light in his eye as Karen put down his pint of beer.

"They're . . . a . . . sure," Karen said.

Sally and Sarah watched with open amusement as Karen tried to cover her embarrassment with off-handed introductions. Fortunately their table was too small for Adam and Riley to sit down, and the men lacked the immediate confidence with city women to suggest that Sally and Sarah join them.

Karen could decline for them the drinks various young men offered to buy, but, as the evening progressed, they had to decline offers to dance themselves. They were finally talked into a game of darts and were inexperienced enough to seem acceptable.

"If they're staying with you," Adam suggested, "why don't we take a couple of cases to your place?"

"This is all the party I can handle tonight, Adam," Karen said. "I've been working, remember?"

Reluctantly the men turned away.

"I can't believe this," Sarah said, getting into the car. "I haven't had to beat off the troops since high school!"

Back at her cottage, Karen was surprised and oddly gratified by their expressions of approval. She had almost forgotten her own first delight in the place with its homely, comfortable furniture, its shelves of books, driftwood, and sea shells, its large stone fireplace. Now, though it was late, she built a fire as if it were her habit, and she remembered that the couch made into a bed for which there were sheets and blankets.

"No wonder you haven't told anyone about this!" Sarah said. "You'd have all of Vancouver over here every weekend."

"And that's the water right out there," Sally said, peering through the night-darkened window.

"I couldn't believe it when you were just standing there in your ferry uniform," Sarah said. "This is so un-you."

"Why do you say that?" Karen said.

"I didn't think you'd ever wear trousers. And two jobs? Peggy won't believe it. It would be easier for her to believe you were shacked up with one of those guys at the pub."

Karen turned away as if distracted by some domestic concern to avoid exposing her consternation.

"Oh, Sarah," Sally said, "you make it sound as if we're on a spying mission for Peggy."

"I know you're not," Karen said quietly. "If she were at all curious, she'd come to see for herself."

"Are there any women on the island?" Sally asked.

"Oh sure," Karen answered casually.

"There didn't seem to be all that many at the pub," Sarah said. "I mean, where's your social life?"

"That's the social life here. And fire practice and the ferries. You can't expect it to be like the city."

"How often do you come to Vancouver?" Sally asked. "We couldn't find anyone who had seen you."

"I don't go," Karen admitted. "When I need something in town, I go to Victoria."

"Are we as bad as all that?" Sally asked gently.

"No," Karen said. "It was just that I realized you were all Peggy's friends."

"Only because you always took such a back seat," Sarah protested. "Nobody could really get to know you."

"Well, Peggy couldn't stand any competition, could she?" Sally asked.

Karen felt the faint tug of that old requirement to defend Peggy against the charge of egocentricity which, if it had some justice in it, was usually prompted by jealousy of Peggy's good looks, money, and charm. It was no longer necessary for Karen to display that steady loyalty. If she hadn't learned to live alone, she had learned to live without Peggy.

Reluctant as she was to have these two in her house, prying at the edge of her loneliness, what they had just revealed to her gave her new confidence. Then, as she lay in her own bed, listening to the quiet sounds of their lovemaking punctuated by the popping and collapsing fire, she felt her defenses burning away like her very skin. Even here in her own house, she was alone in the cold and dark while two people she hardly knew usurped the center.

Milly also lay alone in the dawn-resisting night. She was bleeding great clots of blood as she did every month now. The human body didn't manage its seasons as prettily as some dying trees. In their final season they bloom extravagantly to throw one final mighty shower of seeds before they stand shorn of life and yet newly useful to the crows, ravens and eagles perched on their bare branches to survey the scene below.

Sometimes Milly speculated about being born into an earlier time when she would have gone on having children, so many of them that she would not have had the time or mind to be disappointed in them individually. At least her body would have felt useful. So briefly in the whole span of life had it been an object of desire and an ornament of power, so briefly even childbearing for all these bleeding years.

"Tumors," the doctor had told her. "Fibroid tumors, not malignant, but they should come out."

A hysterectomy. She was to be delivered of her sex. Why did she mind? Why did she keep putting it off? Milly wanted something in her life to end naturally. Nothing did. You didn't even any longer see in an obituary "of natural causes." Either the cause was not mentioned or it was cautionary, "of lung cancer," "of heart disease," "of AIDS." So it was redundant to think of coming to a bad end. Everything, everyone did.

It wasn't sex Milly missed or even human company. Her humiliations were easier to bear unobserved, and without interference she was imaginatively self-indulgent. The terrible loss for Milly was her power to attract because in her day she had been able to stop a man in his tracks, turn him round ten times and head him off in any direction she pleased. What were any of the trophies of that power — the jewels, the fur coats, the expensive holidays — compared to the power itself?

Milly hadn't been a beauty. She had seen how beauty could age and still charm. Henrietta would go on managing that to her last days. Milly had never been charming. She had simply been a woman men had wanted and wanted badly. Well, some men, and perhaps those weren't the kind to marry.

Forbes hadn't lied to her. For years he really hadn't been able to live without her. Then he could — only because he couldn't live without another woman. Milly could always have lived without him, but not in the comfort she enjoyed and he provided. Even at the beginning — and how could one help feeling it? — there had been a small measure of contempt in her affection for Forbes. Passionate men are as dependent as small children. But she'd never mocked him with it, nor had she taunted him about his thinning hair and bulging stomach. His own power didn't lie in his aging body but in his pocketbook. Milly had always had a healthy regard for that until it provided her with no more than subsistence in this summer shack well out of the way of the life Forbes continued to lead.

Milly struggled out of bed and walked carefully to the bathroom. So much in the habit of the experience, she was still shocked at the amount of blood. She was terrified of making a mess, sure she would be blamed for some obscure crime she couldn't deny, for they would have the body, hers. She sat on the toilet weak and weeping.

She mustn't put it off any longer, but she couldn't go through it alone. She'd long since given up hope that anything could bring Forbes back to her, concerned and contrite. She would have to ask her daughter to come from Toronto to be with her, just through the operation and the first few days. Once Milly came back to the island, there was plenty of help.

As she settled herself back in bed, she looked at the clock: 5:00 a.m. If she phoned Bonnie now, Milly could catch her before she went to work.

"Oh, Mother, what are you doing up at this hour?" Bonnie asked, concern and annoyance in her voice.

As Milly described her circumstance, she was aware of melodramatizing it. She didn't, for instance, make it clear that the tumors were benign.

"But shouldn't it be done at once?" Bonnie asked. "Isn't it dangerous to wait?"

"I just couldn't face it alone," Milly said.

"Well, no, of course not. You don't mind if I discuss this with Daddy, do you? He should help — financially anyway."

"No, I don't mind," Milly said, as she heard the quality of sound change and knew, even at this hour, there were listeners who would spread the news of her distress from one end of the island to the other.

"Mother, I'm really sorry. It does seem rotten luck."

"That's the only kind there is," Milly said, but her gloom was gone.

For the first time Bonnie had agreed to something without protest, without excuse, without trying to modify the request out of all usefulness. All the moral suasion, needy pleading and even anger Bonnie had been able to ignore before, but not this . . . this mortal power. At forty-five Milly was too young to use it often, but this operation would give her a chance to test a new hold she might have on her children if she used it skillfully.

Milly resisted the temptation to phone her son and say, "I may be dying." But the time would come when she would be as irresistible to her children as she had been to their father. She would not even have to make any effort. She might not even recognize them. Like Henrietta faithful to her Hart, Milly's children would come. Meanwhile, Bonnie was coming, and probably Forbes would pay her way.

Chapter V

Karen woke to the smell of coffee brewing and did not know for a moment where she was or even who she was, a child again secure in the adult command of morning. How long ago could that have been? She hadn't smelled coffee being made since her parents were together. Once her mother had left them, her father reverted to tea though he never drank anything but English Breakfast.

How simply all signs of her timid little mother had been banished from their life and with what a sharp ache she returned to Karen now, not as a separate identity but as that part of Karen which had been so easily banished from Peggy's life.

The brewing coffee didn't call her welcome; it tempted her instead to dress quickly and slip out the back way to go for coffee and a sweet roll at the store where she was expected if not overtly welcomed.

Sally and Sarah would only suppose she was off to her ferry duties and make themselves the more at home. How easy, even mindless that was when there were two of you. Yet why should Karen let them drive her away without even knowing they had? It was, after all, her house, her coffee, and, if she didn't join them, they'd soon be rummaging around in her meager supplies to find something to eat.

"Good morning," Sally said, standing in the doorway of the bedroom. "Could I bring you a cup of coffee?"

"Oh, no thanks," Karen said, running a nervous hand through her hair. "I'll be out in a minute. There's bread in the freezer for toast, but I'm afraid there isn't much else . . ."

"We brought our own," Sally said. "I'm about to cook some bacon."

It was a relief that she wouldn't have to suggest a public breakfast. Though they'd been perfectly well behaved at the pub last night, Karen didn't want to push that luck.

As she dressed, the smell of bacon was a simple pleasure. The fact that Sally, whom Karen liked a good deal more than she did Sarah, had brought it and was cooking it made Karen feel less invaded and taken advantage of.

"This is such a neat little place!" Sally exclaimed

as she dished up breakfast for the three of them. "Do you have to work today?"

"Only at the pub tonight."

"One night of that is about all I can take," Sarah said.

"Imagine: Saturday night by the fire," Sally said.

Karen had not only imagined it but suffered through it until she had learned to escape into work.

"Well, for the novelty of it," Sarah said tentatively.

Sarah was very easily bored, but she managed to make that trait an asset, hanging it around her neck like an invitation or a challenge. Not many women had been able to resist taking Sarah up on it for a night or a month or a year. Nobody lasted longer than that, not because Sarah turned them out but because they finally ran out of ideas and energy.

Since Karen had neither the confidence nor the ambition to distract or entertain, Sarah's charm was lost on her. Sally's hearty good nature and natural hopefulness, in other circumstances, would have touched Karen, but she was wary of anyone so willing to waste her talents on patently incurable lethargy, like deciding to devote your life to curing the common cold. It would be kinder to the community at large if a Sarah and a Karen could be permanently paired, Karen thought ruefully, locking the bored and the boring away together out of harm's way.

"Could you maybe tell us some of the places we ought to see?" Sally asked.

"If you're not working," Sarah suggested, "why don't you show us around?"

"I guess I could," Karen said. "At least it isn't raining."

In fact the sun that morning held the promise of spring, though the wind off the water was sharp as they set off on the beach walk Karen had proposed as the most scenic way to reach a small shore park where a bit of gorse was always in bloom. It was also the way least likely for them to meet other islanders at this time of year, for they inclined to turn their backs on the sea until it was time to gather seaweed for their gardens and get their boats ready to put back into the water.

"I've always heard about the Gulf Islands," Sally said, "but this is the first time I've ever been on one."

"You're such a ski fanatic," Sarah said, "you forget there are things to do on your own two feet."

"What made you decide to come here?" Sally asked Karen.

Karen shrugged.

"Peggy said she thought some of your people were from around here," Sarah said.

Not *family* but *people*; Peggy would have put it that way. She had tried very hard to make Karen exotic, worthy of her taste.

"I just like it here," Karen said. "That's all."

Sarah skidded on a mossy rock, and Sally offered a steadying hand which Sarah then kept in hers. There was nothing really scandalous about two young women holding hands as they walked along the shore, but it made Karen uneasy. The only house they crossed in front of belonged to Henrietta Hawkins, a woman unlikely to jump to conclusions, but Karen cared about Henrietta's good opinion. Why didn't Sally and Sarah understand that this holiday territory for them was now home to Karen? She didn't want it polluted with innuendoes about herself. Surely one of the few rewards of living alone should be the end of defensive secrecy.

"What's the hurry?" Sarah called.

Karen had put a hundred yards between herself and them by the time she was scrambling over the rocks on the beach below Henrietta's house, and she kept right on going, pretending to be deafened by the wind. When she reached the sloping rock shore of the park, she climbed up to a bench where she could sit and wait for them.

Out across the strait, Mount Baker glinted in the sun like a huge helping of ice cream.

"Well, I'm glad there's some place to sit down!" Sarah said, collapsing next to Karen.

A black puppy with large feet appeared on the grass verge above them and began to bark. When Sally laughed at it and clapped her hands, it came skidding down the rock, tail wagging. Just as it reached Sally and rolled over on its back, Red appeared above them, calling, "Blackie! Blackie!" But the pup was far too enamored of its new friend to pay any attention. Red shrugged and came down slowly over the slippery surface.

"I didn't know you had a puppy, Red," Karen called to her.

"Only got her yesterday," Red said.

"These are friends of mine from town, Sally and Sarah."

Red nodded to them and turned back to Karen. "You wouldn't know anything about training a dog, would you?"

Karen, who had never had pets, suddenly wished she did know something about them. She had to shake her head.

"I know a bit," Sally said, as she played tug-of-war over a piece of bark with Blackie. "She's still too young to learn much."

"I want her to be a good dog," Red said earnestly. "I want her to be responsible."

As Sally settled to discuss a training program, Sarah withdrew her attention and focused instead on Karen.

"Well, have you gotten over Peggy by now?"

"She wasn't a disease," Karen said, trying for a lightness of tone.

"Not everyone would agree with you," Sarah said wryly.

"So bad-mouthing Peggy is still a local sport."

"She certainly never deserved your sort of loyalty."

Blackie, suddenly bored with the conversation between Sally and Red, bounded over to Sarah and Karen.

"I wonder if I should get one of these," Karen said, reaching down to the tumbling puppy. "Maybe Red and I could learn together."

"Are you interested in her?" Sarah asked in surprise.

"Interested?" Karen repeated. "I like her. On this island, friendship isn't a lost art."

These people were no more friends of Peggy's than they had been of Karen's. If she hadn't yet made real friendships here, at least her connections with people like Red and Hen were based on the good opinion she had of them.

"Dogs have always been more reliable than lovers," Sarah said, amused.

"Milly," Henrietta said, putting down her coffee cup, "what have you got against that young woman?"

They were sitting in Henrietta's living room and had been watching first Karen and then two young women they didn't know make their way across Henrietta's boulder- and log-strewn beach.

"I don't have anything against her," Milly replied. "I simply say, 'birds of a feather flock together,' and, unless I'm very much mistaken, those two women are queer or gay or whatever the term is these days. Have you ever seen Karen with a man?"

"She's with young men all the time."

"Of course, but trying to be one of them, making a fool of herself at fire practice, working for the ferries."

"She's not the first woman to work on the ferries," Henrietta protested.

"Have you ever taken a good look at the others?"

This was not the sort of conversation Henrietta liked to be involved in. More and more often recently she found herself regretting the time she spent with Milly, but then she thought, poor soul, having to go through the change on her own and now facing an operation. It was no time to think about drawing back.

Henrietta remembered herself very well at that age, the long hours of irrational weeping. The grief had seemed to her real enough at the time, even when Hart could neither understand nor sympathize.

He had always been patient. Of course he couldn't feel the loss of those babies as she did. They had never been anything but her miscarriages to him. He could have understood if her grief had been for Peter, sixteen years old when a drunk crossed the line and killed him two weeks after he'd passed his driver's test. She did grieve for Peter, of course, and would all her life, but he'd had a life of his own, however short, which those others had not. Her dying womb, hemorrhaging month after month, held all those past failures within it.

"It's a hard time," Henrietta said to Milly, abruptly returning to their earlier conversation.

"Did you have a hysterectomy?" Milly asked.

"No."

"At least it was natural for you then."

"A natural disaster?" Henrietta mused.

"Well, it's the first thing that's made my daughter sit up and take notice."

"Oh, and wouldn't you rather they didn't?" Henrietta asked. "Part of me dreads Hart Jr.'s visits. He always wants to *do* something, and there's nothing to be done. I'd much rather he'd just be getting on with his own life and not worrying about me."

"I *like* being worried about," Milly asserted.

"I'm here after all," Henrietta offered. "I can take you in and visit you and bring you home. Between us, Red and I can give you all the nursing you need."

"I know," Milly said, "and I am grateful. But it doesn't hurt Bonnie to think about someone else for a change, particularly her mother!"

The coffee pot was empty, and Henrietta didn't offer to make another. She was taking Miss James to the pub for lunch, and she wanted time to tidy up before she left. One of Milly's real virtues was that she was quick to pick up such signals and good-humored about them.

"I'll be going along then, Hen," she said. "You are a comfort, you know. Whenever there was anything wrong with me, Forbes was no earthly use. He called me 'Dred' when I was pregnant. He thought it was funny."

"I've never heard a good joke about a pregnant woman," Henrietta said as she fetched Milly's coat.

"And that's the pain you don't forget," Milly said.

The unhealed wound in Milly was humiliation, and Henrietta knew no cure for it. She was afraid it was like arthritis, which simply got worse. Physical pain was easier to be resigned to, and one never had the illusion that sharing it around might lessen it. Milly did really hope that by humiliating other people she might get some real relief. She might be abandoned by her husband, neglected by her children, but at least she was white, at least she wasn't a pervert.

"Come in and have a sherry," Miss James said.

Henrietta accepted the suggestion, which was ritual. In Miss James' small living room she could hear well enough Henrietta's shouted comments; once they got to the pub, Miss James was reduced to talking.

The sherry glasses were crystal. All of the few things Miss James had were good, but none of them looked out of place in her modest cottage. Miss James practiced a kind of elegant simplicity Henrietta admired and secretly aspired to if great old age were to be her lot. But Miss James had been free never to acquire beyond her own needs and to give away what she no longer wanted.

"How's Sadie getting along?" Miss James wanted to know.

"Very well, I think," Henrietta reported in a loud voice. "Dickie's friends are being wonderful. I did tell Riley they shouldn't be too generous with the gin or we'd have another fire on our hands."

"She isn't still on about Red, is she?"

"No, I think she's forgotten all about that. I wish Red would."

"Did you know Red's got herself a dog?"

"No!"

"She was here to show it to me this morning," Miss James said. "A little bit of a thing at the moment, but it's going to be a good-sized dog."

"Is that a good idea?" Henrietta asked.

"Oh, I think so," Miss James said, and she smiled. "It makes me think Red may live long enough to learn how to be young. She's very serious about it, of course, but nobody can help enjoying a puppy, not even Red."

Henrietta found herself trying to imagine Red living here with a dog.

"She'll have it trained before it moves in here," Miss James said, either reading Henrietta's mind or simply on the same track. "I've changed my will."

"I'm glad of that for Red. If we're not the only family she's got, we're all she'll admit to."

"I asked her the other day if Red Smith was her real name because I wanted to mention her in my will. I thought I could say that much. She said as far as she knew it was, except that Red was a nickname for Scarlet. Her mother must have seen *Gone With The Wind* and then decided it was too much. Or Red did it herself."

"Scarlet!"

"Smith's more likely to be made up, but I don't think that should cause any trouble," Miss James said. "Anybody could say Red's the one I meant, whatever her real name is."

"Is she frightened of being found, even now?"

"I wouldn't be surprised," Miss James said.

They had finished their sherry. Henrietta helped Miss James on with her fur-collared coat and watched her settle her fur-trimmed hat with the aid of a mirror in an inlaid frame hanging just by the door.

"I had an old aunt," Miss James said, "who said to me, 'Lily Anne, you can choose to be poor; just don't be shabby.' "

"Did you choose to be poor?"

"I chose to defy my daddy," Miss James said in a pure Virginia accent, "which amounted to the same thing. But poor's never been the real word for the way I've lived. I've never wanted for anything."

Henrietta looked forward to their hour at the pub when Miss James would tell stories of her life as a teacher, never more than a few years in the same place, always moving on until she seemed to have been nearly everywhere, even up to Alaska. It was when she came back down the inland passage and visited Victoria that she'd discovered the Gulf Islands and decided to retire on one of them. She had bought this little house years ago, but she hadn't come to live in it until she was well into her seventies. She liked to say she'd be teaching still if her hearing hadn't gone.

Milly supposed she would have to let Hen take her into the hospital. Otherwise her own car would be in town, available to her daughter for gallivanting around to see her own friends, to see her father, making a holiday out of what Milly wanted to be a hard and demanding vigil. But Milly disliked how often Hen managed to catch her up in good deeds. Now she would become one of them. Henrietta didn't have real friends. People for her were projects like Red and Sadie and old Miss James. Even her husband was no more to her than a twice weekly duty. Henrietta lost interest in people without needs. Without this operation to involve herself in, she would probably be losing interest in Milly, who had noticed how often Hen simply dismissed her, as she had this morning.

Milly hated Saturdays, nothing but the opera to listen to on the radio, nothing to watch on the one channel her TV picked up. Though the bleeding had stopped and the afternoon was sunny, she felt too weak to go out for a walk. But by dinner time boredom had conquered her fatigue. One more game of solitaire and she'd go mad!

Though it was extravagant on her limited budget, Milly determined to treat herself to dinner at the pub. She could sit at one of the small tables so that no couple could take pity on her and join her. How Milly hated those talkative wives glad of any company to distract them from their resigned, doggedly eating husbands. But the few garrulous husbands were even worse, with nothing in their brains but jokes and facts, among which it was hard to distinguish what to laugh at. As for the young men, Milly flinched at the thought of being treated as Sadie was — a worn and blowsy drunk to be humored along. What a sorry state her life was in when even such company as she would find at the pub was better than her own.

That Karen Tasuki was working tonight. Milly watched her with speculative interest, and, when she came to take Milly's order, Milly decided to probe a little.

"Where are those friends of yours?"

"Friends?" Karen repeated.

"The ones I saw walking on the beach this morning, the two holding hands."

"Oh, just friends of friends here for the weekend," Karen said, obviously trying to distance herself from them.

"Where are they staying?"

"With me . . . just until tomorrow."

"Why aren't they here at the pub?"

"Oh, they brought their own food."

"I don't suppose a place like this would appeal to them," Milly suggested.

"They were here last night," Karen said. "Are you ready to order?"

"You needn't take offense."

"I'm not," Karen said, looking around. "It's getting pretty crowded. I don't really have time to chat."

Milly ordered a small fish and chips with a carafe

of white wine which, after she'd finished her meal, she could go on sipping for a couple of hours if she felt like it.

There were more weekenders here than usual, as sure a sign of the coming of spring as snowdrops or crocuses. How young and affluent and healthy they looked, some with winter-holiday tans, their jackets and Scandinavian sweaters no older than last Christmas. If their children had come to the island with them, they were left at home with spaghetti and the choice of a hundred channels on their dish-wired TVs.

Fifteen years ago there had been no pub, and dishes were still in the future. When she and Forbes came over with all three children, Milly had to cook, and the kids were thrown back on such old-fashioned entertainments as cards and jigsaw puzzles. City-spoiled and restless for their friends, they hated to come this early in the year. Once summer arrived they were happy enough to be here, part of a gang of summer children who didn't mix much with the locals, though her son Martin would remember Dickie John.

In only fifteen years, Milly wanted to call over to those young people, *you'll be just like me, an old crow in an empty nest.* And in another fifteen years I'll be just like them, Milly mused, as two old widows came in together, not friends so much as sharers of complaints about their health, their children and their pensions. She could imagine that future as she couldn't have imagined this future for herself fifteen years ago. Then, life beyond children was going to be South American cruises and trips to Europe.

74

Why under these circumstances Milly didn't long for death she didn't know. Even the taste of this very good fish and chips, which Karen had delivered like a bowling ball, could cheer Milly until she defined such pleasure as living for her food.

"Why's a good-looking girl like you sitting all by herself on a Saturday night?"

He was Chas Kidder, a classmate of Forbes, who had bought a place here not long after they had.

"Not waiting for my prince to come, I can assure you," Milly said wryly.

"Well then, maybe I'll do. May I join you?"

Milly nodded. "What brings you here so early in the year?"

"Better than staying home and fighting with my wife," he answered flippantly. "How are you, Milly? I mean, really, how are you?"

She knew better than to think Chas was genuinely concerned. That tone, that emphasis, that eye contact all came from a middle-management course on how to fire people without pain.

"Just as you can see," she replied, knowing she'd been skillful with her rouge as well as her eye make-up.

"Never better, eh? I saw your ex the other day, and I can't say the same for him. A girl that young isn't becoming to a man his age, makes him look old and foolish. 'You know you've traded down, don't you?' I said to him."

"And he knew you were jealous," Milly said.

"No, Milly, I'm not. All he's asking for are bills and back trouble."

He signaled Karen and put a possessive hand on

her arm as he ordered. Chas was the kind of man to make a clear distinction between responsibility and appetite.

"She's a waste of your time," Milly said when Karen had left the table.

"I'm sure of it," Chas said good-naturedly.

"She's not interested in men."

"I never believe that about a woman unless I get it firsthand," Chas said and laughed.

Milly had never realized just how humiliating it was to have the man you were with try to fondle a waitress. She wanted to get up and leave, but she couldn't sacrifice half a carafe of wine and be more of an embarrassment to herself than to Chas.

"How's your wife?" Milly asked.

"Oh, tired of me, Milly. I'll have to work myself into the grave. If I ever retired, she'd throw me out of the house."

"That's a long way off in any case," Milly said in a kindlier tone.

"Fifteen years," Chas said.

He was, like Forbes, five years older than herself, and he was seeing more realistically into the future now that the children were gone and not blocking his view.

"She said a funny thing to me the other day. She said in a way she envied you because you were young enough still to make a life for yourself."

"What's a life for yourself?" Milly asked wryly. "Well, I'll never have to cook brussels sprouts again. There's that."

"You know, I like my wife," Chas said. "I don't really think she likes me. Men don't seem to wear as well somehow. I can't imagine living with one. How do women manage?"

"Don't ask me," Milly said.

"Don't you really think you're better off?"

"Better off?" Milly asked, incredulous, "in my 'sixty-nine VW, in a house not meant to be lived in in winter, twenty years away from the old age pension?"

"You'd rather marry again?"

"Certainly not!" Milly said. "I'm not *that* hard up."

When they had finished dinner and their wine, someone began to play the piano, and two guitars were being taken out of their cases.

"I'm not old enough for the sing-along," Milly said, getting ready to go.

Chas reached over and took her check.

"Thank you," she said.

"My pleasure, Milly," he said and made an effort to rise to his feet.

She supposed he would drink until closing time and then try his luck. Milly was certain Karen would not disappoint her, nor would she disappoint Chas all that much. He was the sort of man to marry, and Milly couldn't abide him.

Chapter VI

Chas Kidder was drunk at the end of the evening and clumsily direct in his approach to Karen.

"You're old enough to be my father," Karen said.

"Is Milly right about you then? Don't you like men?"

"No friend of Milly's is a friend of mine," Karen said, anger overcoming her fear.

"Don't you?" Chas demanded again.

"Don't she what?" Adam asked, belligerent himself by this time of night.

"Ah, nothing," Chas said, giving Adam a friendly jab in the arm.

Karen saw how old Chas Kidder really was, how easily a younger man could deflect and defeat him. She thought of her father who didn't have to try to pick up young women in bars because he had his pick among his college students.

In fact, Karen didn't much like men though that had nothing to do with her being attracted to women. She felt sorry for women who were attracted to men, whether they liked them or not. But, as she drove home, hoping that Sally and Sarah were already asleep, Karen admitted to herself that there weren't many women she liked either.

Sally was asleep, but Sarah sat by the fire smoking a joint. The smell gave Karen an instant headache, which triggered her worst memories of social failures in Peggy's world.

Sarah offered her a toke. Karen shook her head.

"You don't, do you?" Sarah said quietly. "I forgot."

"Why should you remember?"

"I would have made friends if you'd let me, you know," Sarah said, her tone mildly reproachful. "I always used to admire you. Maybe envy's a better word."

"Me?"

"You and Peggy were together longer than anyone I knew. People get tired of me."

"Peggy got tired of me," Karen said.

"She didn't," Sarah said. "You could see through her, and she couldn't stand it."

"That's not true. Peggy's a better person than most people give her credit for."

"She said the only reason you stayed for eight years was that she paid you to do it."

"That's not true!" Karen cried.

Sally stirred and opened her eyes. "You're home. Oh, Sarah, do get rid of that stinking thing. That's why I've been having such horrible dreams."

"It's getting harder and harder to find friends with bad habits," Sarah said, butting her joint.

"I've got to sleep," Karen said.

But she couldn't. She didn't trust Sarah's judgment, but her view of what had happened confronted Karen with the fact that she had no view of her own. She had simply accepted Peggy's. What else could she have done? She could hardly have said, "I am not boring!" It hadn't occurred to her to ask, "Do you really mean that?" She had seen Peggy willfully hurt other people with dismissive judgments but always as a defense against an attack she saw, or thought she saw, coming. Could she really have thought that Karen stayed on only for the free ride? Might Karen have simply gone out and found a job? Peggy hadn't given her that option. Anyway, she would have hated it. Peggy needed to feel generous. She needed to feel in control.

I didn't see through her, Karen thought. *I didn't even see her clearly.* Karen did not want to go over it all again now. It was over, and Peggy wasn't anyone she needed to understand. She needed only to understand herself, to know that she would never again, under any circumstances, be dependent either financially or emotionally on anyone. Sally and Sarah would be gone tomorrow. For the first time the idea of being alone was a relief.

* * * * *

Henrietta awoke both exhausted and restless after a day in town. Increasingly often now, she had a sense of living her life on hold, "spinning my wheels" was Hart Jr.'s expression for it; yet why it should be so she didn't understand. She had no great plans in abeyance. Living life from day to day was what she had always done. It was hard to see Hart in his present state, but he was well looked after, and it was a job beyond her physical strength. She did not look forward to his death, for, even as he was, he was her anchor. She had no appetite for the drift that freedom would bring.

But if there really was a plan to this life, these last years of Hart's life might have better been allocated to Peter. Yet Peter might have been badly damaged rather than killed, and so perhaps Hart was living out a limbo his son had been spared. If you could just know that, if you could see the use, then not so much of life would seem such a terrible waste. Henrietta could not quite convince herself. Suffering so isolated people that it was hard to believe they might be doing it for each other. Henrietta could certainly understand why you'd want to believe that.

I'm like a three-year-old, she thought as she got dressed, *still asking why, why, why of God, a bored grown-up whose attention is almost impossible to get.*

When she remembered Red was due this morning, her tiredness lifted. She was always better off with her attention focused on someone else.

The puppy bolted through the door ahead of Red, nails clattering across the linoleum of the kitchen

81

floor, eager and then suddenly cautious, backing up against Red's legs.

"This is Blackie," Red said. "I had to bring her, but I'll tie her up outside."

"I've heard about you," Henrietta said, offering her hand to the puppy to sniff and then to lick, while Red refastened her leash.

"I just more or less have to put up with her for another month until she's old enough to learn to behave," Red said.

There was a faint blush of color under Red's usually very pale skin. *Scarlet,* Henrietta suddenly remembered and was surprised at how the name didn't suit Red so much as describe some new life in her face, a pilot light glowing that hadn't been there before.

"What made you decide to get a dog?" Henrietta asked when Red came back from tying Blackie up.

"For company," Red said, "and I want her to be a watchdog, too."

Red's answer to putting her money in the bank? Often Red took Henrietta's suggestions and turned them to her own purposes.

The puppy began to bark, outraged at being shut out and tied up. Red frowned.

"She needs a shoe," Henrietta decided.

She went to Hart's closet. She'd thrown out all his old gardening clothes, but she had not been able to get rid of clothes he might wear into town; yet going to the theater or a concert was as much beyond him as mowing the lawn. She ought to decide what he should be buried in and dispose of the rest. She took one of his oldest black dress shoes.

"Oh," Red said, "isn't there an old slipper?"

"He might still need those," Henrietta said.

"But somebody else could get wear out of this."

"Just this pair," Henrietta said, "I'd rather give to the puppy to chew. I'm sure Hart would, too."

Reluctantly, Red took the shoe out to her indignant dog.

"Now don't get any fancy ideas," Henrietta heard her say, "about chewing anything else as good as this."

For the moment, Blackie was pacified. The shoe was substantial enough to be a friend or an enemy or a teething comfort.

Henrietta watched Red as she came back inside. "You know, you're looking awfully well these days. I think you're finally putting some flesh on those bones."

"I've been meaning to tell you, I'm pregnant."

Of course she was. The moment she said it, Henrietta greeted the fact as something she already knew, but she didn't know what to make of it.

"I want to be," Red said. "I want a baby."

"And the father, does he . . ."

"I want to have it just by myself," Red said. "I can take care of it."

"I'm sure you can," Henrietta said. "Have you been to see a doctor?"

"I don't want to be fussed at about it," Red said firmly. "I know what to do."

"You get a puppy."

Red grinned. "Partly. By the time the baby's born, Blackie will be old enough to help."

"Dogs can be jealous of babies."

"That's why I got a bitch. They're less likely to be, and I can train her."

Only when Red had turned her attention to her chores did the questions and concerns clamor in Henrietta's head. The baby's illegitimacy concerned her socially rather than morally. How would Red's other employers react? Milly, Henrietta supposed, would enjoy being intolerant, but she was about to need Red's help rather badly, and Red might keep her pregnancy from her for a while. About Miss James Henrietta wasn't as sure. She might take it in her stride, or she might be grievously disappointed in a young person whose independence she identified with and admired. Sadie no sooner made a surprising entry into Henrietta's mind than Henrietta knew why she was there.

It was Dickie's baby! How could Red not even have bothered to go to his funeral? Had he forced her? Surely, if she'd been raped, Red wouldn't want the child. Sadie . . . she'd be sure to know. Would she blame Red the more or could she be glad of a grandchild? Henrietta couldn't imagine Red tolerating such a grandmother for her child.

The whole island would know. How did Red think she could handle all that disapproval, all those claims? By ignoring them, of course, by isolating herself and the child, with a dog for a companion! If only Red would talk like an ordinary human being, share her fears, her plans, Henrietta might be able to help her, to defend her against criticism. Well, if Henrietta didn't know it was Dickie's baby, she couldn't say, and that would be Red's logic. Not liking to lie herself, she wouldn't ask anyone else to do it for her.

At lunch, Red was distant, and Henrietta didn't try to raise the topic of her pregnancy again though

84

she was bursting with advice about diet and exercise. She had to remind herself that, just because her pregnancies had been like illnesses, there was no reason to assume Red's would be. She didn't drink or smoke — she said there were less expensive ways to kill yourself. When Henrietta offered her a second helping, Red raised a warning eyebrow and then accepted.

"I'm going to take care of myself," Red said then. "You don't have to worry."

"Will you promise me, if you need anything, you'll say?"

Red nodded.

"Will you let me help get things ready for the baby?"

"My mother whored to keep me in good clothes," Red said. "This is going to be a thrift shop baby."

"Is she still alive, your mother?" Henrietta asked cautiously.

"She's in jail," Red said.

"And your father?"

"She never said," Red replied. "She probably didn't know."

Henrietta could not tell what emotion Red masked with that indifference of tone. These were facts Henrietta had long since supposed, and so they came as no shock to her. Her only concern was to treat this fragile confidence in a way that would encourage Red to say anything she needed to.

"I turned eighteen last fall," Red said. "Nobody can touch me."

* * * * *

Milly, having seen her gynecologist to tell him she was finally resigned to the operation, was irritated to discover that, because it was elective surgery, she would have to wait for a hospital bed. Forbes, with all his real estate deals, had always thrived on the policies of the Social Credit government, and, while Milly thrived with him, she supported the Bennett dynasty, though she had always wished they all looked less like petty criminals. Now that she lived in genteel poverty and couldn't bribe her way to the front of the line, she was less sympathetic with the budget cuts which had created the shortage of hospital beds.

"I don't know when," she had to tell her daughter when she phoned.

"How can it be elective surgery?" Bonnie demanded.

She didn't come right out and accuse her mother of lying, and anyhow Milly hadn't lied. She had simply said "tumors" and let Bonnie suppose what she would. But Bonnie was losing her original sense of urgency and complaining about difficulty at work if she didn't know when her mother would need her.

"Maybe you should ask Martin," Bonnie said. "He's not that far away."

"What earthly good would Martin be to me?" Milly demanded. "Anyway, men can't ask leave for their mothers' hysterectomies."

"The whole economic system would be in less danger of coming to a halt if Martin took a few days off than if I did," Bonnie said.

"It's not his place," Milly replied.

"You begin to sound like a R.E.A.L. woman!"

"When wasn't I a real woman?" Milly demanded.

"I mean R, period, E, period — oh, never mind. Just let me know as soon as you can."

"Will your father pay for your ticket?"

"Yes. And he said he'd send roses," Bonnie said.

If he does, I'll send him my womb in a jar, Milly thought, but she didn't say so. Both Martin and Bonnie had made it clear how little patience they had for her hostile complaints about their father.

"Of course he's a bastard, Mother," Martin had said to her. "We all know that, but your pain gets tedious."

"It's tedious to me, too," Milly had snapped.

The thought of Martin at her hospital bed did not inspire confidence.

Bonnie, though she did what she could to hide it, had a gentle streak. Milly was surprised when she had left home to work rather than to get married. She hadn't seemed to Milly the adventuresome girl she apparently was, working for a travel agent in order to get trips to all sorts of exotic places which were only old brochures in the lost future of Milly's life. Maybe Bonnie had a point in seeing the world while she could. Milly was more envious than glad for her. Whoever thought living through your children could be a pleasure? Not even Henrietta seemed to, though no doubt she'd pay lip service to the idea.

Milly picked up the phone again and dialed Henrietta.

Red answered the phone and said, "She's resting."

"Well, she doesn't sleep!" Milly protested.

Henrietta picked up the phone in her bedroom and said, "It's all right, Red."

"I didn't mean to disturb you," Milly said, "but I've just been talking to Bonnie. Now that the damned doctor can't set a date, she's not so sure she can get off work."

"What about your other daughter?" Henrietta asked.

"I have no idea where she is," Milly said flatly. "Nobody does."

"Oh, Milly, I am sorry. Should I have known that?"

"It's not something I remind myself of if I can help it," Milly answered.

"We can manage, just ourselves, if we have to," Henrietta reassured her.

Neither of Karen's parents corresponded with her often. Peculiarly, though they had been separated for years, their letters to her nearly always arrived within a day or two of each other. Karen wondered if her parents communicated with each other about her, their one child who had not made them one flesh but was a symbol of the alien each felt in the other. Her father professed pleasure in her blue eyes, but he was clearly shocked, again and again, to find them in his daughter's face. Her mother never commented on the color of her daughter's skin. Of her hair, her mother had said only that she was lucky the fashion now was straight.

Their two letters had been in her pocket all day, and Karen determined to use her evening off at home answering them. She also wanted this evening to repossess her cottage. She would build a fire for herself and find good music on the radio. Then she would cook herself a real meal and eat it from a plate at the table. She wondered if people like Henrietta and Miss James ever got into the habit of eating things straight from the pot or frying pan. It would not comfort her to think so. She imagined each of them setting standards for herself to be maintained in company or in solitude. And that was what Karen intended to do.

Her mother's letter came from a health spa in Mexico. As far as Karen could tell, her mother hadn't had a fixed address for the last eighteen years. Sometimes her address was a hotel, usually in a large city, but for months of every year she was at one health resort or another in Europe, in the States, in Mexico. She never wrote of being ill, but she sometimes said she was feeling better. Karen wondered if she suffered from some kind of nervous disorder or was a secret drinker. Every two or three years her father presented Karen with a plane ticket and a letter of credit to visit her mother, once in London, once in New York, once in San Francisco. He spoke of them as trips to broaden her experience of the world rather than to maintain a relationship with her mother. Karen wondered if he actually chose the places and sent her mother to them for that purpose.

Karen supposed her father still supported her mother, but maybe she had money of her own. Karen knew nothing of her maternal grandparents. Perhaps they were dead, or perhaps they had disowned their daughter for marrying out of her own race. All such questions went out of Karen's head in the presence of her impersonal and timid little mother. The simplest communication was so awkward and embarrassing that neither of them attempted more than agreeing on the activities of the day.

Her mother's letters were much easier to deal with. She had a certain flair for describing the places she was in, and there were even occasional flashes of wit. The mother of those letters could have been a charming companion, and Karen sometimes indulged in the fantasy that her mother really was this entertaining and amusing person rather than the woman who had infected Karen with her own tense and defensive shyness.

In her letters to her mother, Karen was aware of creating the same sort of fantasy daughter. She saved up little vignettes from the pub and from the dock without ever making it clear that she actually worked in these places. For her mother's benefit she had begun to learn the names of the trees and flowers native to the island, of the sea and shore birds. She took a certain tender pleasure in describing a very shy pair of variegated thrushes that hid in the ferns under the great cedar trees at the head of her path all through the winter. They were as large as robins but prettier with their flashes of black and white and orangy red.

Writing to her father was another matter. He was her Parent, all too real and quite articulate in person or on paper. He had been being patient with her for the last nine years, waiting for her to decide what she was going to do with her life. Of her relationship with Peggy he had said, "If you're going to be someone's live-in help, you might as well come home. I could put you to better and more interesting use." At that time he had just accepted a college presidency in Ontario and was feeling the lack of a wife. When Karen had come to the island and found first one job and then two, he said, "You go out there to declare

your independence and immediately become a slave."
He wanted her to accept the real bondage of graduate
school to make something useful of herself. He was a
job snob for whom simply working for a living was
not good enough.

To be fair to him, once he had passed judgment
on whatever she was doing, he didn't exert pressure
on her again. He was even on occasion unexpectedly
supportive. When she had told him she wouldn't
marry ever, he said, "Why should you? Very few
people are suited to it." It was an attitude which
rationalized his own life, but it was convenient for
Karen, too. She assumed her father was aware of the
nature of her relationship with Peggy and simply
chose not to discuss it.

In her letters to him, she was never descriptive or
amusing. She was always trying to account for herself
without being too obvious about it. And to flatter
him, she always asked his advice, not about anything
really important, but about her car or the virtues of
various savings plans. She was a dull, disappointing,
and not even dutiful daughter.

Karen slammed down her pen. Why did she have
to live her life as a failure in other people's
imaginations? She liked her jobs, both of them, and
they were useful in their own basic ways. She was
learning to live alone, a task that mightn't seem
difficult to either parent for whom it was a natural
choice. How much easier to be someone like Red,
apparently found under a cabbage leaf, entirely on
her own.

This was a night the sea lions were never going
to stop barking. The sound of them out there in the
pass was friendly. If she had a dog making half that

racket, she would be expected to do something about it. It was better to live in proximity to all that boisterous life being responsible for no one but herself.

But what of desire? As pain and shame lessened, their anesthetic effect also could begin to wear off. She did not want her body to betray her into need. She would rather take a vow of celibacy.

Chapter VII

It was raining on the daffodils Milly had planted in a happier time. She was waiting for Henrietta to pick her up and take her to town on the morning ferry. The bag she had packed was very like the one she had carried with her three times before. But on those trips Forbes had bustled her out of the house and settled her into the car like a great fragile egg. He had liked being a little frightened for her; it intensified his sense of dependence and ownership. At those times the phrases "my wife" and "my child" tasted sweetest to him. He had left Milly precisely to avoid this sort of bitter parody of the past, this mortal beginning. A man with a full head of hair didn't have to face aging as long as he put distance between himself and the wife of his youth.

"I wish you bald!" Milly muttered and understood the ambition to become a witch, for only a witch could defeat the vigor of Forbes' hair.

Martin would fare less well, for Milly's father had been bald. Martin's was altogether a more modest masculinity, and perhaps he wouldn't feel it necessary to refuse middle age. He was so tardy at being young that Milly often wondered if he'd get around to marrying at all. She was not impatient for grandchildren though she assumed she'd have to have them eventually.

How on earth was she to go on living with nothing of her own to look forward to but physical breakdown, old age and death?

"Your lovely daffodils," Henrietta said as Milly got into the car.

"Drenched," Milly grumbled, for the sight of Henrietta's glowing white hair, set off by an aquamarine scarf, made Milly's own fading into age drabber still.

"It's supposed to clear later in the morning," Henrietta said.

"Bonnie can get to the hospital by noon tomorrow," Milly said, "so there's no reason for you to stay overnight."

"It's easy enough for me to do," Henrietta said.

Of course, it would be. The Hawkinses' Vancouver friends had rallied around Henrietta after Hart's strokes. Forbes' friends had rallied around him, though Milly had heard he wasn't welcome in some

94

circles with his child bride. Milly wasn't welcome anywhere.

"It would only make Bonnie wonder why she had to make the trip if you were there," Milly said.

"Just as you think," Henrietta said in a tone which warned Milly that "just as she thought" was not something she could indulge in for the whole trip; Henrietta was preparing to be firm with her.

"Good morning, Karen," Henrietta said with genuine friendliness.

In the passenger seat, Milly could risk silence. She had her three dollars ready.

"Good morning," Karen replied, her greeting narrowly focused on Henrietta.

Chas Kidder had phoned Milly to say, "Only thing I found out for sure about that waitress is that she doesn't like you any more than you like her." Such gratuitous malice was something Milly hadn't become used to no matter how often she was its target. An abandoned woman was like a dog you kicked when the real object of your wrath wasn't available.

Milly didn't *dislike* Karen. It was just that she didn't seem clearly enough one thing or another. If she was a Jap and wanted to be one despite blue eyes, she shouldn't mix with white people, even trying to foist off that disgusting seaweed as a *contribution*. Forbes used to say of all the foreign restaurants that had sprung up all over Vancouver — Japanese, Chinese, Korean, Vietnamese — that they were run by a bunch of refugees trying to make poor peasant food exotic. "White folks eat meat," he'd say with a mock Southern drawl. When they went out, Forbes always ordered steak.

"The only reason," Milly said as they waited in

95

line to board the ferry, "young people on this island are vegetarian is that they're too poor and too lazy to buy meat."

"Well, they think it's better for them, too," Henrietta said.

"Rationalization," Milly judged. "You know, I heard one of them say the other day that we weren't meant to eat meat because we're descendants of vegetarian apes! Next thing you know they'll be saying that's why we shouldn't drive cars!"

Henrietta laughed. "Most of our opinions don't bear examining, do they?"

"Most of theirs," Milly corrected. "I was told a horse doesn't pollute the environment. 'Horse shit!' I said, 'If I may quote my late husband.' "

"There are only a few extremes," Henrietta protested. "And they're very young. Look at what's left of our hippy population. They all have jobs. Most of them belong to the PTA."

"You side with the young because you didn't have enough of your own to be overwhelmed by them," Milly said. "One or another of mine always had a better way of doing things, a reason to criticize. I learned I had to shoot 'em the minute I saw the whites of their moral eyes. You take that Karen. She doesn't know her place; she should be put in it."

Making such statements was like putting a green walnut into Henrietta's mouth. Occasionally the taste overcame her manners and she spat it out. This morning her struggle for tolerance was plain on her face. But blander conversation wouldn't be the distraction for Milly that she needed.

All the while Milly carped and baited, another part of her mind was acutely observing the earlier

96

spring dawn, the washed brightness of the arbutus leaves; even the sound of the tires on the wet pavement had a tart freshness. And now here, as they pulled out on the dock ready to board, half a dozen eagles played high in the clearing sky, remote from the hoi polloi of gulls, the emerging sun glancing off their common beauty. She could not help being reminded of how much she had loved this island before she had been marooned here, and she knew it wasn't true that she'd go back to Vancouver in a minute given the opportunity. Aside from her own relative poverty which would make it impossible, aside from the shame of her abandonment so obvious to everyone there, there was simply this island, and it would break her heart never to see it again.

"I'm afraid," Milly suddenly confessed.

Henrietta reached over and took her hand. Had Milly's mother ever been so candidly comforting? Milly wouldn't have let her, and she was surprised at herself now, her hand safe for the moment in Henrietta's.

The vulnerability of that confession and the simple gesture it required freed Henrietta's sympathy from her impatience. She had to learn again and again that unkindness was commonly a mask of fear. Of course Milly was afraid. Who is not, going under the knife? And she was a relatively young woman to be so suddenly and dramatically redefined.

There were a lot of articles these days about a woman's loss of her sense of worth when a breast was removed, the visible scar there where the breast had been. Not much about menopause dealt with the shock of a hysterectomy, the mourning a woman must go through for the loss of her womb, marked only by a fine thin scar at the pubic hair line, if Milly's doctor had been correct when he told her she could still wear a bikini when it was over. All that men understood was the cosmetic loss. Breast amputation was more traumatic for them. The invisible mutilation meant nothing to them.

"You will finally feel better for it," Henrietta said, "but nobody should expect you to be glad."

"Bonnie will," Milly said gloomily. "You can only be utilitarian about your body when it has its uses."

Henrietta understood that. Hart's body now did nothing but prevent him from dying, a stubborn damaged thing which could still lumber his spirit with life. Oh, and she wanted it to and did not understand why simple flesh could be so dear.

At the hospital, they discovered that Milly was assigned to a single room.

"I can't have that!" Milly protested. "I can't afford it."

"It's paid for," the nurse explained.

And there on the window sill were a dozen yellow roses.

"I don't know how he's got the gall!" Milly exclaimed.

"He's doing what he can to help," Henrietta said.

"Do get out now, Hen, will you?" Milly wailed.

Though Henrietta spent an hour with Hart at least twice a week, his physical appearance always came as a shock to her, her memory having sealed over the facts and healed her image of him between visits. Wholly accepting what had happened to him and who he was now might make visiting easier, but it would rob her of his companionship in her mind for all the time she was alone. She didn't lie about his condition even to herself, but she put it out of her mind.

Only when she was buying ice cream did she remember that the day before yesterday he wouldn't eat it, had pushed her hand away like a petulant child as she tried to feed it to him. Was it the ice cream he didn't want or the fact of her feeding him? He couldn't feed himself, and his speech was too impaired to communicate more than an occasional negative like "no" or "bad." His constant mood was irritation which could flare into anger when he had the energy. Maybe he was tired of peppermint. She bought a second pint of strawberry. If he didn't like it, the other patients would.

Hart shared a room with a man whose last name was Clay. People there called him Clay, the way Milly called her husband Forbes. With Milly it was a rudeness. In the nursing home, where first names and terms of endearment were ordinarily used, that last name sounded respectful. Clay was some years older than Hart and entirely bedridden, but his mind was still functioning. When he put his teeth in, he could make himself understood. Clay, in many ways, looked out for Hart, coaxed and encouraged him, called a nurse to head off impending trouble. Henrietta tried not to think what a purgatory it must be for a man like Clay to share all his waking hours with Hart.

She would have made more of an effort to be a

bright spot in Clay's day, too, if Hart hadn't been so plainly jealous, not as a man is jealous, more like a small child confronted with a new sibling. Hart didn't know who she was, but he wanted all her attention.

Henrietta tried to compare this experience with Hart to the mothering of a child still inaccurate at feeding itself, in command of only a few words, at risk of falling with every upright step. A child at that stage is not often content. Everything is struggle and frustration.

Hart didn't want either kind of ice cream, and Henrietta felt absurdly rejected. At least a child's negative declarations of independence, however momentarily irritating or even wounding, were positive signs of development. Hart's rejection of even that ordinary pleasure was a defeat.

"Is he eating other things?" Henrietta asked as she turned the ice cream over to the nurse for other patients.

"His appetite isn't good," the nurse admitted.

Henrietta returned to Hart and sat quietly by him as he dozed in his wheelchair, his mouth slightly open, drool spilling down onto the collar of his robe. If she hadn't known who he was, she wouldn't have recognized him. She felt relieved of her own need of his company, this anonymous old man who did not want her mothering encouragement.

Of course he didn't. He had to teach himself how not to eat, not to speak, to practice indifference to the functions of his body which he could no longer master, and therefore indifference to those around him so addicted to life still that they could not help getting in the way of his dying. Even to soothe him was to betray his purpose.

100

When her hour was up, she did not rouse Hart to tell him she must go. Clay watched her put on her coat.

"You're a good woman," he said to her.

Was all that was left of goodness being able to go without saying goodbye?

"Thank you," Henrietta said.

It was a slow evening at the pub. The few senior citizens had come in early to eat their small portions of dinner, and most of the young men had finished a final beer before going home to eat. Only Adam and Riley still sat at the bar debating whether to have another drink or tonight's special, a seafood platter of local scallops, shrimp, halibut, and salmon.

"Eat first," Karen encouraged.

When she came back out of the kitchen, Red was sitting by herself at a small table, and outside Blackie could be heard complaining.

"Maybe I could find her a bone," Karen suggested.

The cook protested that there must be a policy against canine customers, but Karen reminded him that even children could be served if they stayed outdoors, and he reluctantly produced a large knuckle of soup bone.

"I don't want to spoil her," Red said doubtfully.

"That or drive everybody else crazy," Riley said, for Blackie's yaps of protest had set Adam's dog to howling in the closed cab of his truck.

"Go on," Karen encouraged. "Take it out to Blackie."

"Dumb name for a dog," Adam said when Red had gone outside.

"You be nice," Karen said. "Red hasn't come in here for a long time."

"Nobody's missed her," Adam said, rearing back on his barstool to display his shoulders.

"I have," Karen said fiercely. "And it's a public place, not yours to take over."

"You don't own it either," Adam retorted.

Before Karen could answer him again, Red was back at her table. She wanted chowder and bread.

It made Karen uncomfortable, with the pub nearly empty, to have Adam and Riley sitting side by side at the bar in sullen silence while Red ate her solitary meal. In order to underline her solidarity with Red, Karen poured herself a cup of coffee and sat down at Red's table to drink it. She was glad of an excuse.

"I really came in to ask you a favor," Red said as she finished her soup.

"Sure," Karen said.

"I want to learn how to drive."

"You want me to teach you?"

"Yeah."

"My car's an automatic," Karen said. "If you want to get an old clunker, you probably ought to learn to shift."

"No, that's okay. I'm not going to buy anything. I just want a license."

"Hen's car is automatic," Karen remembered, "if she ever needed you to drive that."

"Mrs. Forbes' is, too," Red said. "I didn't want to ask her, and I was afraid I might scare Mrs. Hawkins to death."

"It isn't hard," Karen assured her, "nothing like

102

training a dog if Sally knows what she's talking about."

"That was nice of her," Red said. "I liked her."

"Have you got the drivers' manual?"

"No," Red said. "Do I need one?"

"Yeah, and I can pick one up for you in Victoria tomorrow."

"Any chance of coffee over here?" Adam asked; he would usually have helped himself.

"Sure," Karen said, getting up.

As she set cups up and poured them for Riley and Adam, she said, "I like you guys better when you're human."

"You might try it yourself," Adam suggested. "Ever phoned yourself up to see how busy you always are?"

"Hey, that's a new one on me," Riley said.

"Right out of the late movie on TV last night," Karen said.

"Why always watch it alone?" Adam asked.

Karen shrugged and turned away. Adam didn't usually pressure her in this way, but, since Sally and Sarah had been here, he had begun to test her. She wasn't sure how to handle it and didn't want to. She had worked at being one of the boys for a year, and she wanted it to stay that way.

The ferry parking lot between sailings was an ideal place for Karen to teach Red the basics of driving. They agreed to meet there on Wednesday and Friday mornings between the 8:10 departure of the ferry to the mainland and its arrival back at 10:20. Without a gearshift to manipulate, Red was confident enough for the road after the first hour, and she drove them to the store for morning coffee.

It was an older crowd who gathered here, the first place where you might learn who had dropped dead at the bridge table last night, whose daughter was pregnant, or who had taken the money yesterday at the golf course. Over the months Karen hadn't exactly been accepted here. She was more friendly with the younger women who worked behind the counter than with the other customers, but by now they expected her. The lack of greeting when she arrived with Red surprised her. Red seemed to take no notice.

"No coffee?" Karen asked as Red waved a hand against the cup Karen was about to pour her.

"I'll get juice," Red said.

"How long do you have to live on this island before you turn into a health freak?" Karen asked amiably.

"Until you get pregnant," Red answered.

Karen glanced around, but no one seemed to have heard the remark. She led them to an isolated corner before she asked almost in a whisper, "Are you?"

Red nodded.

Karen still did not dare pursue the subject until they were back in the car.

"What are you going to do?"

"Have it," Red said.

"Do you want it?"

"That's why I'm pregnant," Red said.

"When?"

"In about four and a half months."

"You're going to do it all by yourself?" Karen asked.

"Only way," Red said. "Don't you ever think about having a kid?"

"I'm gay," Karen said, surprised at how undefensively it came out.

"I know," Red said, "but that doesn't make any difference."

"I suppose not," Karen admitted, "but I haven't thought about it since I was a kid myself and just assumed I'd have to. I don't think I ever liked the idea."

"I don't like the idea now," Red granted. "But there's no other way I'd get a baby."

"Are you afraid?"

"Sometimes, a little bit, but mostly I think about how it will be when I have the baby."

"Do you think people are going to give you a bad time?"

"There'll be nothing new about that," Red said. "I told Mrs. Hawkins. She was all right."

"She would be," Karen said.

She wanted to go on to say that she'd do anything she could to help, but it was too early in this new stage of friendship to make offers for the future. What Karen had to do now was build Red's trust so that she could just assume Karen's help when the time came.

Blackie, tied to the toll booth, was hysterical at the sight of them as Red steered the car through the narrow pay lane and out onto the wide blacktop with its reassuring margin of error. Karen used the marked lanes to teach Red the finer points of steering.

"If there had been a car in that lane," Karen chided, "you would have taken off its fender."

While Red practiced, the dog continued to bark.

"I'm going to kill that dog before I get her trained," Red said finally.

"That's what I'd think about a crying baby," Karen confessed. "Better you let that dog develop your patience."

Red looked at Karen and grinned. "You're right."

There were two cars already lined up at the toll booth. Rat had gotten out of his and was playing with Blackie by the time Karen and Red reached the booth. In the car, his wife nursed their baby.

"You guys ever want a baby sitter?" Red asked, looking in the window.

"Can't afford it," Rat's wife said.

"No charge," Red said.

Karen was unlocking the booth and worrying that Red's sudden interest in someone else's baby would give away her secret. But it would give itself away quite shortly. Red should probably tell people before they could see for themselves.

"This is going to be a fine dog," Rat said wistfully.

"I hope so," Red said, struggling to untie Blackie while the dog jumped to lick Red's face.

"Do you know anything about babies?" Rat's wife asked.

"I'd like to learn," Red said.

Rat had taken his wallet out and was paying Karen. Then he turned back to Red before he got back into his car.

"Who's the lucky guy?" he asked amiably.

"Guy?"

"Woman starts getting interested in babies . . ." Rat said and shrugged.

"Better move it," Karen said to him. "You've got a lineup behind you."

"See you Friday," Red said as she started back up the road, Blackie dancing at her side.

As Karen watched her go, she wondered why she hadn't already noticed for herself that Red was pregnant, or had her hips always been that ample? Peggy had called Karen a hypocrite when she denied that she noticed other women's bodies. But she just didn't. She wasn't attracted to bodies. It had been Peggy's confidence which had drawn Karen to her, not her undeniable good looks. But Karen had come to wonder if confidence was like make-up, something you put on as you did your public face, which wouldn't survive an honest scrubbing. Red's manner was as innocent as her face of the will to attract. Karen's new interest in her body was not erotic any more than was the sight of the breast of that young nursing mother. Karen was moved by such involvement in instinctive life. Was she abnormal to feel no such desire for herself?

Karen turned away from that question impatiently. She had had enough of internalizing the world's judgments. She had heard Milly Forbes say having babies seemed to be a new vogue on the island. Anything Milly said could be discounted, but this outbreak of babies was like any other sort of epidemic in which people got caught not so much by instinct as by propinquity. Well, not Red. Red was as deliberately having a baby as she had made her vegetable garden.

The dog was part of the scheme, as was learning to drive, though Karen didn't see quite how that skill fitted in with Red's planning if she wasn't going to buy a car. She wasn't a borrower.

Abstracted as she walked down the dock to lower the ramp, Karen made only casual note of those in line for trips to the other islands. But her glimpse of Henrietta Hawkins driving off the ferry startled her out of her own musings. Henrietta's face, despite the bright color at her throat, was as white as her hair.

Chapter VIII

The lower half of Milly's body was like an empty sack, not only without womb but without bowels or kidneys. That empty sack filled up with pain until the nurse arrived to puncture it with a needle and the pain leaked away, only gradually to fill the empty space again. At its peak pain was her reality which only the nurse could invade, but each time it seeped away, players waiting in the wings came onto a stage of several levels where they competed for her attention. Those actors on a level with Milly were gentle with her, wiping cold sweat from her face, asking her easy, pointless questions she could ignore. On platforms off to the side and above her, the actors demanded that she take part in the drama or pass judgment on it, which she hadn't the strength to do. Yet, when she failed them, she could follow them off their stages as if she had traveling vision, see them change out of their costumes while they complained about her as if they really were her children and not professionals at all.

The actress playing her lost daughter Nora was the most irritating of all, throwing incomprehensible accusations at Milly like, "I didn't run away; you did. You're lost. Can you tell me where you really are? Can you? Then what does it mean that you don't know where I am?"

"But I don't," Milly whined, turning restlessly against the attachments which both anchored and seemed to suspend her body.

Martin was sometimes on the first level, a face strained with concern, but more often he was up on his own platform turning it into a pulpit from which he gave pious speeches on his old theme: "Mother, your pain is tedious."

He had no idea what pain was, she realized, no concept at all. He seemed to her such a silly, innocent boy, standing up there mouthing his platitudes like an actor, which he was. It wasn't really Martin up there delivering Martinish lines.

Nor were those two on the other side really Forbes and his child bride. They didn't take any notice of her at all, and they didn't really do anything but gaze into each other's eyes, but Milly was alarmed that they might. She told the nurse several times to warn them that she could see them perfectly clearly even when they went offstage, and she wouldn't tolerate any of their sordid carryings-on.

Then gradually the pain rose onto that busy landscape like a blinding sun until she could see nothing else. She came to welcome it and to be reluctant to have it taken from her, for without it she had to live victim to all this posturing and moralizing from people or actors or whoever they were who had no conception of what she was going through.

"Of course we do," the Nora one said. "We are what you are going through."

Bonnie, on Milly's own level, said, "There's nobody there, Mother. It's the drugs they're giving you for the pain."

If Nora and the others were mere hallucinations, why were they in so much sharper focus and so much more audible than Bonnie, who faded in and out like a badly tuned FM station?

"This is a bit more than you bargained for, poor darling," Henrietta said through a great deal of static. Was she addressing Milly or Bonnie?

Then all the stages were empty, even the one by her side. Milly was alone and terrified. She did not know where she was. She wanted her watch, but she could not find it. She could hear something like the magnified beating of a heart as slow as a funeral drum, and she knew it was her own. It had been taken out of her body. Someone must have found its key and wound it up like a great clock to tell other people the time. Milly hadn't agreed to that. They'd gutted her like a chicken, left the cavity of her body open to these swelling winds of pain which were overcoming everything, not just the irritating sorrows of her life but life itself.

"I'm not ready!" Milly tried to cry out, but she had no voice.

"You should get some rest now," Henrietta said to Bonnie. "Your mother is through the crisis."

"For a while there I was afraid she didn't want to live," Bonnie said, "that she was just letting the infection take over."

Henrietta heard a trace of guilt in that fear. Though Bonnie was staying with her father, she obviously wouldn't be able to talk with him about such things.

"Would you like to go for dinner before you go home?" Henrietta suggested.

"What about your ferry?"

"I can stay with a friend and go back in the morning."

"Then yes, please."

Henrietta took Bonnie to a quiet little seafood restaurant which had survived the Hawkinses' years away from town. It had been a favorite of Hart's who, unlike most men, liked fish.

"The first few days went so well," Bonnie said, "and then just all of a sudden that high fever . . ."

"A bit of very bad luck," Henrietta said, handing the menu to Bonnie.

"What has she got to live for?" Bonnie asked.

"Why, all sorts of things!"

"Her only real interest is hating my father,"

112

Bonnie said gloomily. "She isn't really interested in any of us."

"She wanted you here," Henrietta reminded her.

"Not *me*," Bonnie replied. "She's an emotional baglady, you know. She treats us all like things she's left behind. But she doesn't want it to look that way. So in a crisis she rummages for one of us to make herself look like a mother — to the doctors and nurses."

Henrietta hoped some of this anger was exhaustion and relief.

"I shock you, don't I?" Bonnie asked.

"No," Henrietta answered. "Your mother isn't an easy woman. And she's been very unhappy."

"You sound as if you think that's over."

"She won't have the energy for it for a while at least," Henrietta said, smiling. "She might get out of the habit."

"I'd make more of an effort to come out and see her, but I don't really think she wants that. Oh, she says she does, but then she behaves as if I'm there to check up on her, to spy for Dad. And I can't really tell her Dad doesn't give a tinker's damn about her."

"He sent her roses," Henrietta said.

"He paid for them and for the room because I asked him to. He's very easy to guilt-trip these days."

"How is it for you, staying there?" Henrietta asked.

"Oh, it's all right, I guess," Bonnie said tiredly. "I don't see any point in resenting him for being happy, but it's a hard contrast seeing Mother the way she is. I'd never marry."

Henrietta thought of Red and of Karen. In her own day not marrying would have been a disgrace.

113

No amount of evidence against marriage would have changed that. Though Henrietta had had several opportunities to marry before she accepted Hart, she still felt that old gratitude to him for her social legitimacy. She had it still even though he was no longer there to reinforce it.

"Marriage can be a relief and a joy," Henrietta said, but she was embarrassed by such platitudes and grateful that their dinners had arrived to distract them.

While Bonnie retrieved clams and mussels from their shells, Henrietta could observe her at leisure. She was probably better-looking than Milly had been, but she had none of Milly's artifice and magnetism. It wasn't necessary to look at Bonnie though pleasant to do so. Her brown hair, indifferently cut, was clean and full of copper lights, and the color was coming back into her face with each bite of food.

"This was such a good idea!" Bonnie said.

"Are you in touch with your sister?" Henrietta asked. "Can you let her know about your mother?"

Bonnie, her mouth full, shook her head.

"Does your father know, or your brother?"

"No. The closest I've come to Nora in the last years is in Mother's hallucinations."

Henrietta was too tired for the amiability necessary to impose on a friend for the night. Instead she indulged in the rare luxury of a modest hotel room. She never came to town without an overnight case, so she could settle herself comfortably. The anonymity of such a room was strange to her, used as she was to the personal clutter of other people's spare rooms, either a foldout bed in a den or a deserted child's room prepared for visits of grandchildren. Without so much as a cast-off crossword puzzle book or a stuffed toy, the hotel room invited melodramatic speculation: call-girl murders, drug deals. It wasn't opulent enough for such carryings-on. It could have sheltered only the less ambitious: the traveling salesman, the visiting relative not close enough kin or too modest to sleep on the living room couch, even perhaps a tourist. It was difficult for Henrietta to think of Vancouver as a tourist town even though it had recently survived Expo. It was still too much her home, though she had no intention of living here again.

The island, perhaps because she had had to live there so long alone, seemed to belong to her in a way the city never had and never would. Most of its pleasures were now beyond her. She would never learn to go out alone at night to a film or concert. And shopping, except for Christmas, only reminded her of how much she already had that should be given away. Though she still had close friends here, the old crowd was faltering into age. Too much of the gossip was of death and dying. On the island, it was easier to be close also to the young.

But I fail them, she mused.

"What has she got to live for?" Bonnie had demanded.

Henrietta should be able to explain clearly why such a question was absurd. Once you stopped thinking of life as something requiring a destiny, you could accept it as the realer miracle it was, meaning inherent in every moment of it. Humiliations and defeats could blind you for a while, but for most the healing process did take place. You woke up one morning simply glad to be alive, to be part of human

115

consciousness. Well, all right, you finally did have to learn to die, but there was really no point in moving from the crib to the coffin, as if shunning sleep in the great bed of life would save you pain or give you power.

The bed Henrietta lay in seemed larger and emptier than her own because it was unfamiliar. Did those widows who traveled round and round the world, teaching themselves to sleep in strange beds alone, need to learn something that was still ahead of her?

She thought of Milly finally sleeping peacefully, the fever broken. She thought of Bonnie lying alone under the roof of her father's new happiness, refusing such illusions for herself. And Red who had decided to tolerate no heart beating next to her own except her child's. Henrietta would not think of her husband except as he had been all those years beside her in the kingdom of the present, which perhaps no one learned to value enough at the time.

Her light sleep, often broken by the sudden bangings of doors, the sirens in the night streets, left her tense and restless. She got up before dawn, checked out of the hotel and drove out of the city before the morning traffic began. At sunrise, she stood on the tarmac of the ferry terminal facing west so that she could see the first light falling on the dark smudge of island lying out there twenty miles offshore. Then she went into the coffee shop for breakfast.

Henrietta had just had her first sip of Styrofoam coffee and was breaking open her bran muffin when she thought she heard her name called over the public address system. It came a second time, "Mrs. Hart Hawkins."

Who could know she was waiting for this ferry and here an hour early? Well, almost anyone she knew would assume that, if she hadn't made the night boat, she'd be on this one. With only two ferries each way a day, it wasn't all that difficult to track down an islander.

She was directed to a phone.

"Mrs. Hawkins? I'm so glad I've reached you before you left. Your husband died at four this morning peacefully, in his sleep."

Henrietta held the phone away from her ear, stared at it and then slammed it down as she would have with any other obscene call. How dare anyone play such a dreadful trick on her!

She hurried back to her breakfast, but it had been cleared away in her absence. She had no appetite for it now anyway. As soon as she got home, she was going to report that person, whoever he was, a grown man playing with the phone like a naughty child! If only Hart were well enough, he could handle such a thing, his calm and firmness always so reassuring. It was silly to feel as agitated as she did, as nearly violated.

Henrietta sat in her car impatiently waiting for the ferry to unload its passengers from the islands so that she could get aboard, get across the water, get home. Once on board, she didn't leave her car. She was first in line, could be first off. She hummed to herself, tapped the wheel, was vaguely conscious of an urgently barking dog left tied up alone on the car deck. It wasn't kind to travel with animals.

117

Henrietta couldn't see the progress of the ferry, but she had made the trip so often she could guess quite accurately their position by the sound of the engines. There was always a high alarm like an electric sigh just before arrival at the island was announced. Then the great doors swung open, and she could see the houses in the curve of bay, the wooded hill beyond, and finally the dock itself. There was Karen, abstracted, giving her a belated sign of welcome as she drove off the boat and onto the dock.

It was a glorious spring morning. The island wasn't like the city, showy with flowering trees and blatantly overplanted flower beds. You had to keep an eye out for quiet spots of pride, a small clump of daffodils at a front gate, primroses along a path. The wild spring along the road was the moth white of the earliest blossoming berries. In the woods and meadows, wildflowers had to be hunted like Easter eggs.

Once Henrietta turned into her own drive, she had no patience for the secrets of her own garden. She hurried into the house calling, "Hart! Hart!"

Karen saw the last cars onto the boat, repositioned the ramp, and locked up. She couldn't get the image of Henrietta's face out of her mind. Perhaps it had been only a trick of the morning light, an illusion just as the reflected color of Henrietta's scarves was an illusion. Karen could not persuade herself; yet she didn't feel she knew Henrietta well enough simply to follow her home to check on her. Even if Milly Forbes had been at home,

Karen wouldn't have called her. Why didn't Red have a phone? Might she phone Henrietta herself? They'd let her use the phone at the store.

There wasn't any answer. Had Henrietta perhaps stopped to see someone on her way home? Miss James? But if she wasn't with Miss James, it might worry the old lady. Karen got into her car and drove over to the Hawkinses' house, noticing the sign that marked their drive. *Hen & Hart* over *Hawkins.* Residents had been asked by the fire department to mark their places carefully since there were no house numbers, but the cute heterosexuality of a lot of them irritated Karen, this one included. It made her less certain that she should be intruding. She had to remind herself that Henrietta was a virtual widow, there alone, not one half of a smugly nesting couple.

The car was in the drive. The back door stood open. Karen knocked on it anyway. Then she stepped inside. There was no one in the kitchen. She found Henrietta in her living room, staring out at the view.

"Hen," she said gently, "are you all right?"

Henrietta turned an ashen face toward her. "Have you seen Hart?"

"Hart?"

"My husband," Henrietta explained. "I've had such an awful scare — a sort of crank call at the ferry terminal — someone saying . . ."

Karen stood near her, waiting.

"Oh," Henrietta said and stared before her again.

"Saying?" Karen tried to prompt her gently.

"It can't be true, can it?" Henrietta asked, her usually strong voice nearly childish. "He can't be dead."

She was too confused, too dazed for Karen to ask

119

any practical questions, like the name of the place where her husband was or how her son could be reached.

"I'll make you some coffee," Karen offered.

In the kitchen she plugged in the kettle and then phoned the store.

"Get someone to go to Red's and get her over to Henrietta Hawkins' as soon as possible."

Karen wondered about phoning the doctor, but she wanted someone who knew Henrietta better than she did to make that decision. As she waited for the kettle to boil, she tried to figure out what must have happened. The crank call at the terminal must have been the real thing and Henrietta just couldn't take it in. Karen couldn't find any instant coffee. Did Henrietta always make real coffee for herself? Karen unplugged the kettle and started again with the electric coffee pot. She worried about leaving Henrietta alone so long at the same time that she was glad to have the excuse to be away from her. She had always seemed to Karen so sane and strong. Karen's experience with deranged emotional states was limited to other people's sexual anguishes, usually complicated and blurred by drugs or drink, and she had never been any good at dealing with them. She left Peggy to cope. It had been hard for Karen to believe that such behavior was genuine. Peggy had told her not to measure everyone by her own Oriental inscrutability. It was only partly a joke.

When the coffee was finally ready, Karen found Henrietta just as she had left her. Some innate courtesy roused her enough to acknowledge the coffee, but she made no attempt to drink it. Karen had the sense that Henrietta was trying to hide or at least to stay very still, almost as if she had broken bones whose pain could be outwitted if she didn't move.

Finally Red called from the back door, and Karen went to the kitchen to meet her.

"Am I glad to see you!" Karen said and quickly sketched in what she thought must have happened.

Red went in to Henrietta, sat down beside her and took her hand.

"Can you tell me what's wrong, Mrs. Hawkins?"

Henrietta started to speak and then shook her head.

"Do you feel sick?"

Henrietta didn't answer.

"Call the doctor," Red said quietly to Karen.

When Karen had done so, Red directed her to sit by Henrietta while Red went off to phone the hospital in Vancouver. Karen found it oddly natural, even comforting, just to sit there holding Hen's hand.

"You were right," Red said. "They're very glad she made it home. They were worried about her."

Then Red knelt down in front of Henrietta and said directly to her, "I'm going to call your son."

Henrietta didn't respond.

The doctor arrived while Red was on the phone talking with Hart Jr. Karen stayed with Henrietta, leaving Red to explain in two directions at once. Then the doctor spoke briefly on the phone. Finally he came into the living room. He looked hardly stronger than Henrietta, a man semi-retired because of problems with his own health.

"Henrietta," he said gently, "Hart is dead. Your

son is coming. I want you to rest now. I'll give you something to help you rest."

Karen could feel the old hand flinch, but Henrietta obediently rose and let herself be guided into her bedroom where Red undressed her and settled her in bed.

"I've given her a shot," the doctor said as he came out of the bedroom. "She'll sleep now for a few hours. Can one of you stay with her?"

"Yes," Red said, "I'll stay."

Karen looked at her watch. She should leave for the pub in just a few minutes.

"I could come back later," she offered, "and give you a break."

"That's okay," Red said. "I'll just stay on till her son gets here."

"Her husband's been sick so long," Karen said. "I wonder why it came as such a shock."

"She's old," Red said, "and tired. And it's something she can't fix."

"It surprised me," Karen admitted, "to see her like that. I guess I've always thought of her as what I'd like to be when I grow up."

"There aren't any grownups," Red said.

"Aren't there?" Karen asked. "What about Miss James?"

"Old isn't grown up. She made running away into what she calls 'career choices.' Oh, she's a nice enough old bird, I'll give you that . . ."

"You're cynical, Red," Karen accused.

"I don't know words like that," Red said.

"You haven't any faith in the goodness in people."

"Some people are good when they can afford to

122

be," Red allowed. "Most people can't afford that and won't. I don't believe in anything about anybody."

"Then why are you willing to be so good?" Karen challenged.

"I'm not *good!*" Red exclaimed with a laugh. "I'm about to be an unwed mother, remember?"

"There's nothing wrong with that," Karen said.

"That's not what you'll hear at the store or the pub. I'm trash. Even to the likes of Sadie, I'm trash."

"You don't have to listen," Karen said. "You don't have to believe that."

"I don't," Red said. "I don't believe anything about anyone."

"Why are you willing to stay here for Hen, then?" Karen asked.

"I owe her," Red answered.

As Karen drove to the pub, she pondered Red's moral view. It was clearer and more realistic than Karen's own, but it was too simple surely and gave no room for the altruism in some people, which wasn't purely a luxury of the rich in pocket. She was surprised at Red's harsh judgment of Miss James. Of course, Karen didn't know these women as Red did.

No man is a hero to his valet. How peculiarly so many old maxims lay on the rural hierarchy of island life. Karen was their servant, too, whether she sold them ferry tickets or waited on them at the pub, and she had been thinking of them as her betters. The old ones she respected anyway, but not in a social sense. Karen had been raised the daughter of a highly regarded university professor, and she had a college degree herself, which was why her father would think the work she did now demeaned her — or he would if she began to think of it seriously, as a way she

123

could spend her life. You were to make something of yourself so that no one dared to look down on you.

But most ignorant people felt superior to Karen and her father. Even their rights as citizens were at the whim of the government. Why wasn't he angry? Why did he instead want to prove himself good enough to people who should have been beneath his contempt? Red was still just a kid, but she'd learned that she was "trash" even to pathetic drunken Sadie, and she kept her pride. She didn't care what they thought, any of them.

Why should I? Karen wondered. For all the contempt she felt for Milly Forbes, her judgments nevertheless stung. And, if Henrietta Hawkins was friendly, Karen felt reassured of her own value. And was shaken to see that old woman in a state of collapse.

Was she wrong to see her father's vanity exposed in his sexual behavior and therefore to judge his pride in the same way, a false striving of self-serving ambition that would never change the color of his skin or the design of his eyelids? There were people in the camps who had killed themselves. Surely their despair wasn't more honorable than that surviving generation of overachieving super-patriots.

There were simplicities in being a fatherless bastard which Karen both mistrusted and envied. She was learning that the mirror of her own value could not be the face of a father, lover, or child, nor could she find it in the old women among whom she'd been looking for role models. Certainly she didn't want to be someone who perpetually ran away from failed loves, inadequate friendships, and meaningless work until she was so old and deaf that her inadequacies could be blamed on great age.

The healing wound of Karen's pride had begun to itch.

Chapter IX

Milly lay watching the sunlight on the fresh roses which Bonnie had brought this morning. If Milly had had more energy, she might have demanded whether these, too, had come from Forbes, but she hadn't the strength or mind for vexation. She was reduced to passive and basic pleasures. Roses in sunlight, the at first very painful and now just miraculous reawakening of her bladder and bowels. Milly had dealt with her body so long as an aging enemy that it was a largely forgotten experience to be aware of it simply as a servant to her consciousness. She breathed and felt her lungs at work acquiring oxygen for her blood which traveled through her veins carrying nourishing messages. For every conscious effort she made, her body carried out thousands of instructions she was not aware of. She felt amazed by it and grateful.

In birth, the child's body was the miracle. Milly's own, torn and depleted, breasts sore with her first milk, had been something to be pitied — a crude and vulnerable vehicle for life, hardly belonging to her at all, though a vital convenience for the child. And very soon — she had never been able to think how — it would have to be repaired and restored to the uses Forbes made of it.

Now no one else's need pushed at her. She could lie and rest and let herself heal for herself. She didn't resent the nurse's urging her out of bed for the short journey to the bathroom, and, though she didn't yet look forward to the time she spent sitting in a chair each day, she knew she would.

While Milly had been very sick, Bonnie seemed nearly always at her bedside. Now she came briefly in the morning with flowers or a magazine, came back in the afternoon for a real visit and occasionally again briefly in the evening.

"Don't muck up your evenings for me," Milly told her. "There must be lots of old friends you'd like to see."

"I don't," Bonnie assured her. "You were on the way to a party tonight, that's all."

Milly didn't really remember most of the people Bonnie referred to, expecting her mother to be familiar with high school and college friends who had frequented the house and who had often been more

127

charmed by Milly than Bonnie had liked. They had never been much more than a blur of young faces to Milly but when Bonnie had complained at her mother's behavior, her friends became something more of a challenge to beguile. "I'm teaching you how," Milly had said to her daughter.

Instead of complaining that she couldn't be expected, even with full presence of mind, to remember all those callow young, Milly let Bonnie chatter on about them and their affairs until, for lack of other interests, Milly began to look forward to Bonnie's reports like episodes in the soaps. She could probably have watched television instead, but, since she had lived on the island, she was out of that habit. Bonnie, right there in the room with her, was an easier distraction.

"You should do your eyes like that all the time," Milly commented one evening when Bonnie came more dressed up and made up than usual.

It pleased Milly that Bonnie after that came to visit with a careful face, whatever the time of day. It was as if she were a kind of stand-in for Milly until she could rouse herself to prepare her own public face again. She was relieved that Martin had gone away now that she was better, for he would have been a strain on her vanity.

Bonnie asked her if she would like other company.

"Who?" Milly wondered.

When Bonnie mentioned Chas Kidder's wife or Chas himself, Milly declined.

"Hen might come one of these days when she's in seeing Hart."

"He died, Mother," Bonnie said gently, as if such news might upset her mother.

"Well, good!" Milly exclaimed. "I hope Hen packs up and goes round the world on a freighter."

"Would you like to do something like that?" Bonnie asked.

"Oh, I've hardly got the money to live the way I do," Milly said dismissively.

"I get a lot of perks in the travel business, you know," Bonnie said. "I maybe could arrange something."

"I wouldn't have the clothes," Milly said.

"They're not all fashion-plate cruises," Bonnie said.

"But those are the ones I'd like," Milly said. "And anyway I wouldn't want to travel alone."

Bonnie didn't press the issue, and, though Milly didn't take her seriously, she got a new vicarious pleasure in the travel magazines her daughter brought to her.

"What a comfort it must be," the nurse said to her, "to have children like yours."

Milly realized that, in fact, it was. But nearly everything was a comfort to her in these placid days of her returning strength. She did not want to be hurried, and no one was hurrying her.

Then one day Bonnie said, "The doctor thinks you might go home day after tomorrow, if I'd go with you for a week or ten days."

"You can't miss that much work!" Milly protested, who had not until that moment put her mind to the work Bonnie had already missed.

"I can," Bonnie reassured her. "And I'd really like to, Mother."

"But what would you do with yourself on the island? You'd be bored to death."

129

"No, I wouldn't. I always loved it there."

"Did you?" Milly asked, mildly surprised, and then she remembered that she had once loved it there, too. "Nobody your age comes any more," she said.

"I've seen enough people in the last couple of weeks to last me a while," Bonnie said. "I could take walks. I could do a little yard work for you. There must be things you'd like done around the house. And we can just go on visiting. It's been years since we've done that."

Bonnie spoke in a tone wistful rather than reproachful, allowing Milly to remember faintly a time when she had felt companionable with her children before they had begun to witness her humiliation and to tell her all those things about herself that made humiliation even more inevitable. Bonnie had never been brutal to her as the others could be, but Milly had shrunk back even more from her kindness which made it all too clear that she had become an object of pity.

"The girl, Red, said she'd come in as much as I need her," Milly said. "And Hen. But, if you can spare another week, I would like it."

Admitting this wasn't difficult because Milly really was feeling proud of this healing body of hers. It deserved Bonnie's attention and kindness as it did her own. Milly had a peculiar feeling that she and her daughter together would be leaving the hospital with a new life on their hands — her own — and she was free after all these years to give herself that attention and receive it from her daughter.

* * * * *

The rationale for great community effort quite left Henrietta when she was faced with the question of a funeral for Hart.

"Is there really any point?" she asked her soberly concerned son. "For his friends he died years ago."

"He didn't for you," Hart Jr. reminded her.

That certainly was the fiction she had kept up for all these years, but now she had to face the fact that the disagreeable stranger she had visited so faithfully was really her husband, and he was dead, his body lying on a shelf in the funeral parlor awaiting her instructions. Deprived of his company all these years, she didn't want him carried back into the house like a piece of furniture.

"Did he have . . . any wishes?" Hart Jr. asked, this solid, middle-aged banker, being her son.

"Wishes? He would have liked just once to win the salmon derby."

"I mean about what's to be done now," her son said with obvious patience.

"Oh. Not really. He favored cremation generally. But for himself I don't think he cared one way or the other. He used to say it was for the living to bury the dead any way it suited them."

It was hard to call up such information. The Hart who had been so accessible to her for these lonely years had been replaced by a dying old man who could be angry with her for bringing the wrong flavor of ice cream and might have a tantrum at the thought of her turning him into ashes, except that he was dead.

"I didn't bother to wake him when I left the last time I saw him."

"For him, I'm sure that was the right thing," her son said gently.

"We don't know, do we?" Henrietta replied sharply.

Hart Jr. sat unnaturally still. She wanted to shout at him that that dead body was nothing but an embarrassment to her, a sick joke. But she was aware that her feelings were inappropriate.

"I have to give the funeral people instructions this afternoon," Hart Jr. said finally. "And, if there's to be a funeral, I ought to call Georgie."

"She wouldn't try to bring the children!" Henrietta protested.

"No," Hart agreed, "but she'd want to be here herself."

"It's such a big disruption for everyone," Henrietta objected.

"Mother, you've always seen the value in ceremonies."

"Oh," she said, "for other people."

"Well, there are other people involved — friends, nieces and nephews who may want to pay their respects."

"And you," Henrietta said, suddenly remembering. "What do you want done, son?"

"I don't want it to be difficult for you," he said, drawing back from her. "It doesn't have to be a funeral. It could be some sort of memorial service here or in Vancouver."

Henrietta couldn't think where. She couldn't think. She wept, frustrated and angry tears which her son accepted as one of the manifestations of grief. He put an arm around her and offered a box of Kleenex.

"I'm not really falling apart," she said when she

had recovered herself. "I just don't seem able to think, to make decisions."

"Well, unless you have any real objection, I think cremation is the right thing to do."

"The ashes?" Henrietta asked timidly, the idea of them a lot less daunting than a corpse. But ashes were still in need of disposal.

"I could scatter them out in the pass," Hart Jr. offered, "where he liked to fish."

"You hate boats," Henrietta reminded him.

"That's overstating it," her son said mildly.

She could see that he resented her old reflex to protect him from his father's enthusiasms. She was inadvertently reminding him of a way he had been a less than perfect son for his father. What Henrietta would have liked to say to him was how much she admired the grace with which he had always refused to be the focus of all their needs, all their lost hopes for the children who hadn't survived. He had managed to grow up to be himself in spite of all their errors. Hart Jr. hadn't gone fishing with his father not only because he lacked any real interest in it but also because he had no desire to usurp his brother Peter's memory. But one word about any of that would sully his sense of the past.

"Well?" Hart Jr. asked.

"Yes, all right," Henrietta agreed, not quite sure what she was agreeing to except to let him make the decisions.

In many ways by now he was a stranger to her. She didn't know him at work and had had only glimpses of him as a husband and father. But it was right that he should grow away from her into manhood. He was a stranger she trusted.

How unnaturally her husband had separated himself from her until he became a stranger she didn't trust even for ordinary human concern. And dead, that stranger couldn't call up any of the emotions she was expected to feel. Why were the stories of changelings always about children when so often it was the old who were stolen away, in their place such helpless and horrible substitutes?

Your father was horrible, simply horrible! Henrietta wanted to shout and was immediately ashamed of herself.

Why did she have to face this terrible failure of love, this knowledge that she never had really accepted that damaged old man as her husband until he finally managed to die, taking the memory of Hart with him?

"I'll make arrangements for a memorial service, Mother," Hart Jr. said. "In Vancouver, I think. More of his old friends are there. We can provide transport for anyone on the island who wants to go."

He held up her address book and asked, "Could you maybe just check the names of those who should be asked?"

"Half of them are dead," Henrietta said. "I always meant to update it. I never got around to it because it's hard to cross people off."

"What you need is a new book," her son suggested.

"I must try to be some help to you, darling, but just at the moment I have to lie down."

Though they still met in the ferry parking lot,

Karen and Red no longer used the space for driving lessons. Red needed more practice driving in traffic than the island easily provided even when Karen made her feed into the arriving line of cars.

"I can't take you off island behind the wheel until you get your learner's permit," Karen said.

"I know," Red agreed. "But I can't get off island to take the written test until things quiet down a bit: Mrs. Forbes just home from the hospital and Mrs. Hawkins too out of it even to help her son plan a memorial service and Miss James in bed with a cold. I'm running from one to another with no time in between."

"Should I do something?" Karen asked.

"Miss James is the only one who maybe just needs company. But you have to remember to shout or it's no good."

"I know," Karen said, "and I'm not very good at that."

"Practice," Red ordered as she negotiated one of the island's worst curves with relaxed skill.

"Don't think you're good enough at it until you can outguess cars all around you," Karen warned her.

"I don't know whether I'm going to like that or not."

"You probably will," Karen said. "Why not try turning around here? It's safe but nasty."

Karen watched her pupil with some pride. Even her very limited experience in teaching anyone anything had led her to expect odd resistances. In Red there were none. She wasn't reckless. She trusted Karen's judgment both to set and to stretch limits. Perhaps more rare was the relationship between them. They seemed to have no hidden agendas.

"I can't stay for coffee today," Red said. "I promised Mrs. Forbes' daughter I'd go over there."

"What's she like?"

"She paints herself up just the way her mother does. They seem to get along."

"That's hard to imagine," Karen said.

"I know. She's never had a good word to say about her kids, and this one turns up to help like she really wanted to."

"There's no justice in the world," Karen grumbled.

The renewed friendliness in the store also irritated her, and she barely responded to greetings that weren't forthcoming when Red was with her. The lunch soup was mushroom and nearly ready. Karen ordered two servings to go while she drank her coffee. Then she drove over to see Miss James.

Hers was one of the older cottages on the island, most of which had been built by their owners with varying degrees of success. The site for this one was its best feature, up on a knoll on the land side of the road, high enough to catch glimpses of the sea in the winter months yet sheltered by an even higher hill to the weather side of it. Few earlier inhabitants of the island had chosen to settle right by the sea, and having lived at its restless edge for a year, Karen understood the desire to be a little removed from it. Here in Miss James' wild little garden nothing tugged at your attention. It was a peaceful pocket of sunlight in which fragrances lingered free of brine, a place where someone should sit writing poems. But it was empty, and the cottage had the closed-up look of drawn curtains and firmly shut doors.

Karen banged loudly on the back door and then

opened it into a long narrow kitchen that had probably been a back porch before it was incorporated into the house. An unwashed cup sat on the counter by the sink next to a small bowl of withering fruit. The small living room was orderly, dark and dusty. But a modestly promising light shone from the bedroom beyond.

"Miss James?" Karen shouted as she neared the bedroom door.

"Who is it?" Miss James called, her voice resonant with cold.

"Karen," she answered as she entered the doorway. "I brought you some soup from the store. I wondered if you'd like company for lunch."

Miss James was sitting up against a wealth of pillows, her shoulders covered with a densely embroidered shawl. Her cheeks were flushed, her eyes bright with fever.

"How nice," Miss James said. "I do get bored being put to bed like this. The doctor seems to think a sneeze could break a rib, the slightest chill bring on pneumonia. I could as easily die of the doldrums. Red put you up to this, didn't she?"

"She said you might like company."

"She has too many of us on her hands this week. At least the others have children helping out."

Karen liked the mix of irritation and approval in Miss James' tone. She wanted to be more possessive of Red than she knew she had any right to be.

Karen went back to the kitchen to reheat the soup. While she waited, she opened a cupboard to find bowls. The china, though in frugal supply, was nevertheless good. She wondered if it was remnants of family belongings or things Miss James had

137

collected with a fine eye in rummage sales and secondhand shops. The soup bowls were translucent Japanese china, three of them. Into such bowls Karen should be pouring a thin broth with a fine piece of seaweed, a square of bean curd, a little green onion — not this hearty homemade cream of mushroom. Well, she could do that another time. The well-traveled Miss James would not turn up her nose at things foreign the way Milly Forbes did.

"Have you ever been to Japan?" Karen asked as she brought in the lunch.

"No, I bought those in San Francisco before the Second World War it would have been, before the *disgrace* when all their shops were shut down."

"They're beautiful," Karen said.

"Of what little I have, everything is," Miss James said, her taste having been her own for so long that it would naturally seem to her universal.

As Karen looked around, she could see that nothing was makeshift. The bureau was an antique without missing brass or a chip, the headboard of the single bed a gleaming backdrop to the remarkably upright old woman. The one chair in the room, on which Karen sat, made her feel more upright than usual, too. It was a tiny bedroom, uncrowded and uncluttered.

"I assume this is good," Miss James said. "I can't taste a thing, which gives me only the most basic motive for feeding myself."

Karen knew what an effort it was for herself, even with a good appetite, to feed herself a decent meal. But she imagined Miss James' habits of survival were so ingrained that she'd never inadvertently starve herself.

"It is good," Karen thought to say but not loudly enough, and, when she repeated herself, she knew Miss James wasn't sure what she was talking about.

"You seem to be very good at living alone," Karen shouted.

"I've had enough practice," Miss James replied.

"I'm better at it than I was," Karen said, "but I don't think I'll ever really like it."

"It's lost some of its appeal by now," Miss James said. "Nobody seems to disapprove any more. In my day it was quite a balancing act to live alone and stay respectable. Whenever I felt bored or lonely, I could always remind myself how daring I was being. I still do feel daring," Miss James said, and laughed.

"Well, you are," Karen said.

"Red doesn't think so," Miss James said more thoughtfully. "I used to tell her about all the places I'd been, all the different schools I'd taught in. I wanted to encourage her to think about her own life. Do you know what she said to me? She said, 'I wouldn't want to have to keep running away.' That gave me something to think about. I was a runaway, of course, and that took courage of a kind, but the bravest sort of people may be those who can be themselves wherever they are, even at home."

"But you probably have to be a certain sort of person from a certain sort of home to be able to do that," Karen said. "I wonder if Red ever had a nest to be pushed out of or fly from."

"She won't say," Miss James said with mild irritation. "Well, I didn't say either until there was no chance that somebody would send me back."

"Would you like a bit of fruit?" Karen asked.

"What's that?"

"Fruit?"

"No thank you, child. I'll rest now."

Old people, like children, could simply say. Karen took the bowls back into the kitchen and washed up. She thought of Miss James taking pleasure in her own things, the choices of a lifetime. For Karen things were either horribly impersonal or belonged to someone else, like the things she used where she lived now. Was one of the secrets of living alone beginning to accumulate around you what suited and pleased you? She had moved from her father's house to Peggy's, from Peggy's to the welcome clutter of the beach cottage. Karen had never bought anything for her own domestic comfort. She hardly knew what her own tastes were. She might be as bad at choosing furniture as she had been at choosing a lover — selecting a handsome chair which would in the long run give her chronic back pain.

Karen sighed as she put the lovely bowls back among the other treasures of the cupboard. She was coming to understand that if she was to have a life, it must be a deliberate one. The exercising of choice at every level still seemed an exhausting and unnatural business, like collecting stage props before a play could begin. But unless she began, she might wait in the wings of her own life forever.

Chapter X

Henrietta woke from a dream in which she had been frantically pushing that demented old man away from her as he rose above her with the eyes of a rearing horse. She was shaken and exhausted. Even the great cedar outside her window had become a menace. She might be losing her mind.

When she saw her navy suit laid out on the chair, she remembered that Georgie had done that for her the night before so that dressing to catch the morning ferry would be less rushed.

"I can't go," Henrietta said aloud.

In her own voice she could hear the echo of Sadie's refusal to go into the room where the coffin was, her refusal to go to the grave. She herself was not being asked to do either of those hard things. Well-supported by son and daughter-in-law, all she had to do was listen to a few people pay tribute to her husband as he had once been. If she wasn't up to staying for a glass of sherry afterwards, Georgie would take her out to the car, and Hart Jr. would deal with the guests.

How unlike herself she felt, her body forcing her reluctant spirit out of bed when for years she had relied on her spirit to defy her aging slowness. She felt like a tank without a driver lumbering about her room until she happened on her robe hanging from a hook on the door. She put it on, listening to discover whether the bathroom was already occupied.

Hart Jr. was shaving at the kitchen sink, using a mirror still there, put up by his father for just such mornings as this to alleviate traffic in the bathroom. Georgie, whose bones had just begun to define her face, moved around him preparing a breakfast which she'd also set out the night before. There was too much thoughtfulness in Georgie's efficiency for it to feel intrusive. Henrietta was grateful they'd vetoed breakfast on the ferry in favor of local eggs, soft-boiled, and decent coffee at home.

Neither of them looked around as she went into the bathroom or when she came out of it, leaving her a sense of privacy until she was dressed and in as much possession of herself as she could be.

Inspecting herself in the mirror, she knew she should have washed her hair. She reached into her scarf drawer before she remembered that this was not a day for glowing color, but she must have something to cover her aging throat, something to distract people from the lifeless hair and chalky skin. She had one scarf with only the thinnest border of kelly green. It didn't do what she needed, but it was an improvement.

Neither Hart Jr. nor Georgie asked her if she'd slept well. Each kissed her on the cheek, and her son held her chair as his father had taught the boys to do when they were still quite small. The flicker of Peter's boyish presence for a second confused her. Why should it disorient her now when Henrietta alone was used to living in a kaleidoscope of time, her husband and children richly inhabiting her only seemingly solitary life? Hart Jr. and Georgie actually there with her inhibited and distorted her sense of memory, as if it were some demented impropriety she had indulged in. Perhaps it was. Living this day in the shallow present was the only way she could get through it, and they would help her with that.

"These eggs are wonderful," Georgie said. "I forgot what real eggs taste like."

Henrietta liked and approved of Georgie though she was part of the fabric of Hart Jr.'s life that made him a stranger. The moment he had told them he wanted to marry, Henrietta felt a door shut. She had never so much as tried the handle since, and she wouldn't even now when she knew that her son must have a grief of his own for a father who had not been allowed to squander all his paternal love on this remaining son, a son who had taken only what was good for him and no more.

"You must eat your breakfast, Mother," Hart Jr. said to her.

"Yes," she agreed, taking up her forgotten spoon. "I don't seem able to keep my mind on anything."

Georgie buttered her toast for her, so absent-minded a motherly gesture it did not seem condescending. *Take comfort, take comfort,* a voice urged Henrietta. If she could be a good child through this day, she could manage.

At the dock, Hart Jr. got out of the car and walked over to greet a carload of men, young Riley and Adam among them. Homer was driving. Henrietta hadn't seen them so dressed up since Dickie's funeral.

"I wonder where they're off to," she said to Georgie.

"The service," Georgie said.

"For heaven's sake!" Henrietta exclaimed.

But of course they had known that other Hart who had belonged to the Chamber of Commerce, run the bingo games at the Lions' Fiesta, raised money to improve the dump. They somehow could remember a man who had become a fiction to her in these last days against the harsh reality of the man who had actually died and now howled and clawed at her consciousness, insisting on being acknowledged and mourned.

On the boat, they all spoke to her, but then they kept a respectful distance. She understood that they simply wanted her to know that they were there. She had helped them bury their dead. They would help her now to bury hers. But they didn't know, they didn't know who had died! Then for a moment she remembered Riley's young unshaven face when she asked him if he might say a few words about Dickie and how bitterly he had answered her at first. Had the drunken self-destructive Dickie been staggering

144

around in his mind blotting out the friend, the hard worker, the hopeful builder of his own house?

They had all seen Hart helpless before she'd finally been forced to give up his care. Hart Jr. and Georgie had dutifully gone to visit him in hospital when he hadn't the faintest idea who they were. Yet here they all were, ready to mourn his loss without apparent hypocrisy.

The ferry shuddered a little as it moved from the shelter of land into the open water where a spring wind freshened.

"Look!" Hart Jr. said.

Off to the port a killer whale broke the surface of the water, sleek black back, white belly flashing in the sunlight, then another, then another, a whole pod of them out there choosing to escort the ferry across the water to mock the horror in Henrietta's heart.

"He loved them," Hart Jr. said with quiet satisfaction.

Who? Henrietta wanted to demand. *Who?*

The man who had just died cared for no one, for nothing. But Henrietta seemed to be the only one who was required to know that.

Milly was sorry to be too weak to consider going over for Hart's memorial. The only time she and Hen had talked on the phone, Milly was so shocked at her lackluster vagueness she forgot her own invalid state and made some real attempt to cheer Henrietta up.

"You'd think she'd be relieved," Milly said to Bonnie.

"Red said a very odd thing to me about it,"

145

Bonnie confessed. "She said Mrs. Hawkins never thought about that sick old man as her husband until he was dead. Does that make any sense to you?"

"That's Red. She hardly ever says anything, and then, when she does, I usually don't know what she's talking about. Hen went to see him every other day. *He* was the one who didn't know *her*."

"Red said I shouldn't go to see her just yet," Bonnie said. "Mrs. Hawkins was so nice to me when you were in hospital. I'd like to think of something to do for her."

Milly was tempted to tell her daughter that only people like Red called Hen Mrs. Hawkins and Bonnie didn't want to sound like the paid help, did she? But Milly didn't. She'd finished raising Bonnie years ago and hadn't the energy to take such tasks on again now.

"What's wrong?" Bonnie asked.

"Not a thing, Miss," Milly said, "and don't keep trying to second-guess me or read my mind just because I'm your mother."

Bonnie laughed and then said, "I was afraid you'd get grumpy once you got out of hospital."

"And?"

"And you haven't, but it would make me nervous if you didn't tick me off a bit sometimes."

"It's not my fault you're a better nurse than I thought you could be," Milly retorted.

Bonnie laughed again, obviously pleased by the backhanded compliment which was the only sort Milly was good at handing out — and she'd been pretty sparing with those in the last few years.

"I feel so much better than I thought I would," Milly said. "And that's because you're here so that I

146

can stop the minute I feel tired and let you take over."

"Will you know how to do that by yourself?" Bonnie asked, concerned.

"I'm learning, and it helps that I'm naturally bone lazy."

"You?"

"Without an audience," Milly modified. "I was surprised to find out how little I could do in a day without feeling guilty — bored sometimes but not guilty."

"Is it enough of a life here for you?" Bonnie asked.

"I wouldn't have thought so. It's not what I wanted."

"Of course not," Bonnie said.

"But it's what I've got," Milly said. "When you've been as sick as I was there for a while, it leaves some sort of afterglow on everything. I suppose it will gradually wear off, but at the moment it would seem criminal for me not to be glad to be alive."

That was as much explanation as Milly could give for her continuing uncommon sense of well-being. It made her generous in ways she couldn't remember ever being before. She did not begrudge Bonnie her long walks, her friendliness with Red, her occasional beer at the pub. Such venturings, far from leaving Milly alone and feeling sorry for herself, extended her own sense of her life on the island, the real pleasures there were here.

Often, as they sat over a meal, Bonnie would recall a family outing that had been disastrous or comic or wonderful or all three at once.

"Oh, and when Martin broke his arm!" Bonnie

147

exclaimed and they both burst out laughing because he had been so stoically informational, holding up his arm as if it were something quite separate from himself, saying, "I broke it."

"We were awful to Martin," Bonnie said.

"Nonsense!" Milly said. "We treated him like a little prince."

"Like a frog with prince potential," Bonnie amended, and again they laughed.

The night before Bonnie was to leave, she said, "You know, I always used to wish I were a real islander and could stay after Labor Day and go to school here. When you came back to live, I still remembered that kid dream and thought maybe you would feel lucky, too."

"School only goes through the seventh grade," Milly reminded her wryly.

"Would you write to me sometimes?" Bonnie asked.

"Write to you?"

"When we talk on the phone, it feels like we have to do the mother/daughter act for half the island. I'd write to you, too."

"Rash hopes. Rash promises," Milly said gloomily.

"They're not," Bonnie insisted.

Milly put her hand out to touch her daughter's young cheek and said, "I'm going to miss you. I didn't think an operation could be such fun."

"You forget the bad parts," Bonnie said.

In that week of reminiscing, they had both forgotten the bad parts, and for the first time in years Milly felt free to see beyond the past as a place to find mitigating if not vindicating evidence against the charge of failure. It was here on the island that so many of the memories did lie innocent of anyone's wrongdoing. Not only the children but she and Forbes were freer to be outside the social definitions and requirements that increasingly overtook them in town. In Vancouver they had become a microwave family, each on his or her own fast track, until the speed had flung each one out of the orbit of family altogether, Forbes the first to go, and she hadn't even noticed it until he was too far away to retrieve.

Let go the bad parts, her body and her daughter were teaching her. She realized with no little amazement that she was never going to bleed again.

"No," Red said, "I'm not going to throw all that stuff out, Mrs. Forbes. What happens when your daughter comes to visit again? It would be like not having any toilet paper."

"I didn't mean you to throw it out," Milly said. "You could use it."

"Not for a while," Red said. "I'm pregnant."

Milly, usually so casually appraising of other female bodies, could have known that, her eyes easily verifying Red's announcement. In her own physical preoccupation she hadn't noticed.

"You're having it?" Milly asked, incredulous.

"Yes," Red said, "in about four months."

"Without a father?"

"I'm a bastard," Red said.

"You don't have to let a man get away with that, Red," Milly said. "Make him marry you."

"I don't want to be married," Red said. "I just want a kid."

149

"But you can't just have one," Milly protested. "What will people say?"

"What they say already," Red answered.

"Have you told Hen?"

"Yes."

"Didn't she tell you to get an abortion?"

"No," Red said, looking quite directly at Milly with that unreadable face.

"Surely she doesn't approve!"

"What difference does that make?" Red asked.

"Well, she's done so much for you. She's thought so well of you. She's tried to teach you how to lead a decent life."

"Decent," Red repeated.

"She has. We all have. How could you do such a thing? Why would you want to disappoint so many people who've been so good to you?"

"It's none of your business, Mrs. Forbes," Red said, and she turned and left the vacuum cleaner standing in the middle of the hall.

"Red!" Milly called. "You come right back here! You can't walk out just like that!"

The back door slammed. The weakness, which could come over Milly suddenly, kept her from following Red out into the drive. She sank instead onto the living room couch and burst into tears. She couldn't do without Red. She wasn't even strong enough to put the vacuum cleaner away.

When Milly had recovered herself, she reached for the phone to call Henrietta, to demand some explanation for Red's circumstance and behavior. How could Henrietta have allowed it? Then Milly remembered that Henrietta was not sufficiently strong enough to come to see her. Henrietta was as

150

dependent on Red as Milly was. But surely they couldn't be expected to put up with Red's pregnancy without so much as an explanation or apology.

"Don't be a prig, Dred," she heard her husband say. "It doesn't become you."

"Morality isn't supposed to be part of my beauty contest mentality?" she had asked in her most sarcastic tone.

"She's pregnant. I want to marry her."

Nothing priggish about that, of course! Honorable.

Where was the sense of benign well-being she had been wrapped in over these last weeks? Why did she have to face all the hurtful ugliness of the world again? Bonnie had left her much too soon.

"It's none of your business, Mrs. Forbes."

What came into her house certainly was her business, and, if she let Red go on working for her, it would amount to condoning her behavior. Then it occurred to Milly that Red wasn't offering her that option. She had quit. She couldn't be allowed to do that. Red was irresponsible to leave Milly still nearly helpless. Who else could come? There wasn't another young woman on the island trained the way Red had been trained.

Are we all to turn into victims of our own servants? Milly might even have to apologize to get her back. Never!

Karen saw Red off with Rat in his car on the day she was to take her written test. Karen wondered if she'd pass it. Red wouldn't be helped with it. She said she learned things better by herself when they

151

had to do with words. She certainly wasn't stupid, but she'd had so little schooling that Karen worried she mightn't realize what was expected of her. She had been in a bad mood since she'd walked out on Milly Forbes.

"You get gold marks for leaving her alive," Karen had told her.

"Mrs. Hawkins isn't going to like it," Red said. "She's going to say to me, 'Who's to look after her then?' "

"Let her look after herself," Karen said without any sympathy, "until she learns to be civil and to mind her own business."

"She'll die of old age first," Red said, and grinned.

But she hadn't really cheered up. She was a funny combination, short in patience and long in concern for people. She didn't forgive Milly, but she worried about her.

All her ladies, as she ironically called them, were a worry just now. Miss James' cold persisted with a deep phlegmy cough, and Henrietta could be roused from lethargy only by the firmest coaxing and then not for long. Karen would have nothing to do with Milly, but she had told Red she'd look in on both Henrietta and Miss James.

Henrietta hadn't got out of bed.

"Are you sick?" Karen asked, concerned.

"No," Henrietta answered in a voice that had lost all resonance, "I wasn't expecting anyone."

"Have you had any lunch? Could I fix you something?"

"Don't trouble yourself, dear," Henrietta said.

Karen, with a boldness she was just discovering, sat down on the bed beside Henrietta and took her hand.

"You have to trouble yourself now, Hen."

Henrietta patted her hand absent-mindedly.

"Would you like me to help you get dressed?"

"What for?" Henrietta asked.

"It's the wrong question," Karen told her.

She knew from her own experience. There wasn't any answer to it. With no one to urge her, she had lain in bed for days until she had bored herself into getting up, a natural vitality asserting itself. Henrietta was too old to count on that. Karen and Red had determined they would lend her their vitality in turns until she learned to be self-propelled again.

"Tell me what you'd like to put on," Karen said.

"Oh, whatever."

"Then I'll pick one of my favorites," Karen said, going to the closet.

She realized that she knew only the wardrobe Henrietta had for town, that she rarely saw her in the knockabout sorts of things people wore on the island. She chose a rust-colored linen and knew just the scarf Henrietta wore with it.

"No, dear," Henrietta said, shaking her head. "I'm not up to that."

Reluctantly Karen replaced it and looked for slacks and a top. Once she'd helped Henrietta into those, Karen had to put a comb in her hand to remind her that her hair needed attention.

"I've had such a shock," Henrietta said to her image in the mirror.

"Yes," Karen said.

"Nobody seems to understand that," Henrietta said.

"Come out now and sit by the view," Karen said, "and I'll fix you something to eat."

"I haven't any appetite," Henrietta said.

Karen ignored that complaint. Red had suggested a menu of smoked tuna, Ritz crackers and cranberry juice. Obviously Henrietta liked bright colors even in her food and drink. It was a garish little tray Karen carried back into the living room.

Henrietta ate dutifully, nearly automatically, her attention fixed somewhere deep and out of reach. As long as she ate, Karen was content to leave her alone. But once the small meal was finished, Karen determined to rouse her from her torpor. It could become habitual if she was allowed her grieving way.

"Have you heard from your son?" Karen asked.

"He calls too often."

"He's worried about you," Karen said. "We all are. Of course, you've had a shock, and you have to grieve, but . . ."

"I don't grieve," Henrietta said, tears she could hardly have noticed leaking out of her eyes.

"Why are you crying?"

"Because love dies," Henrietta answered.

Karen had no response to that. Certainly her own had, but she had come to doubt that it ever had been love. Fantasy, need, habit: could these in combination actually be called love? The genuine feeling should certainly transcend such things, be ultimately altruistic and, yes, undying.

"Why do you say that?" Karen asked, trying to keep her own urgency out of the question.

"Simply because it does," Henrietta answered. "It's a shame."

The tears continued to find their downward way by the detouring wrinkles of that beautiful old face. It wasn't an idle cliché she offered. She was suffering shame. Karen didn't understand why, since Henrietta had clearly done all she could do for her husband, even long after he had forgotten who she was. No one could fault her behavior as a loving wife. Karen supposed his love for her had seemed to die, but years ago, something she had come to terms with, surely, had come to understand and accept. It wasn't his choice.

Was it ever a choice for anyone? Peggy couldn't have wanted to be bored, could she? *We stop recognizing each other, and love dies.* Karen found herself memorizing Henrietta's face.

Miss James was failing against her will. Unable to hear Karen, that ancient of days turned to her usual solution, but talking started up her cough, and Karen understood for the first time why people with pneumonia were said to drown. There seemed such a shallow space in Miss James' lungs left for her to take air, short gasps of it between fits of coughing. She seemed to be collapsing in on herself, flesh hollowing into bone.

"Should I call the doctor?" Karen asked.

Miss James shook her head. When she had enough breath again, she said, "He's coming later."

"Lie quiet now," Karen shouted, wondering how the deaf could ever be soothed.

She sat very still herself, willing Miss James to rest, and she did, her breathing finally so even that Karen knew she had fallen into a light sleep. Karen didn't suppose it would be like this if you actually nursed the old. You'd have too many patients to give peaceful time to any of them. She could hear her father, if she said she was thinking about nursing as a career, asking her what was wrong with being a doctor. The fact that she was nearly thirty would seem to him more an excuse than an impediment.

She was doing what she wanted to do right now and would get better at it with practice rather than training. Her ambition, as it awakened, was of the heart, and she would listen to that, however indefensible it was.

Red signaled victory as she drove off the ferry with Rat that late afternoon. She had passed her written test and was now a legal driving student who could be taken off island and into the traffic.

Chapter XI

It had been three days since Red had walked out on Milly, and the vacuum cleaner remained in the hall to be climbed over every time Milly went from one room to the next. When she finally phoned Henrietta, Henrietta's voice was so faint that she might have been speaking from beyond the grave. Milly didn't mention Red's pregnancy or complain about being left helpless. In fact, she was more worried about Henrietta than she was about herself, for, though she was still weak — too weak to indulge in the kind of temper tantrum she had had over Red

— she gained new strength every day. The doctor had told her she could begin to drive again at the end of the week, and then she could call on Henrietta and see for herself what was to be done about her collapse.

When Bonnie called to see how she was, Milly didn't tell her either that she'd been left stranded. What could Bonnie do, two thousand miles away, but worry? And Milly wasn't entirely sure that Bonnie would take her side of the quarrel. So recently having enjoyed her daughter's good opinion, Milly wasn't as ready to sacrifice it as she had once been.

Bonnie would probably tell her that a lot of girls were choosing to have babies on their own these days. It was a fact which could hardly go unobserved even on this little island where there were already several mothers married to nothing but welfare. Milly wasn't being unkind when she saw abortion as the only solution — she wasn't one to think the young should have to pay for every mistake. A bit late now, though, wasn't it? So Red should be persuaded to give the baby up for adoption. What kind of life did she think she could provide for a child all alone? That she was a bastard herself was a ridiculous argument!

Hen obviously hadn't the mind to confront Red with such a decision, and Red wouldn't talk with Milly. Could Miss James perhaps persuade her? Miss James was having too serious a flirtation with pneumonia to deal with anything else. But if Red did have the baby and go on welfare, where would they all be?

There were other young women willing to clean

house, but they weren't willing to see themselves in that role. Red took her job seriously and had no social pretensions about being above the work she did. Even having an illegitimate baby was conforming to type, but Red obviously wasn't literate enough to know that a servant so compromised was sent away, whether the child was the master's or the footman's. If Milly didn't exactly want Red to slink away in the night, she certainly shouldn't be allowed simply to brazen it out. Only in a minister's house could a young mother and bastard child be taken in, out of Christian charity, of course, but also because such household labor was all a minister could usually afford.

In the all too loosely structured social world of the island, it was important to set and maintain standards. If it weren't for herself and the Henriettas of this world, there would be no Reds.

Servants who knew their place were such a dying breed they could hardly be found now outside books. In town, professionals had taken over. Milly knew one bridge club which scheduled its meetings according to who had to be out of her house while the cleaners were there. At large parties you often recognized more of the waiters and waitresses than you did the guests because nearly everyone now used the same firm, and those young people were trained to be able to tell you not only the names of the other guests but the name of your host, if it was one of those parties you'd gone to just because your husband thought it was important to be seen there. For small dinners you began to depend on places like the Lazy Gourmet, a shop that would fill up your own casseroles and baking dishes which didn't have to arrive at the house until fifteen minutes before the guests did.

Henrietta was old enough never to have lived that way. Milly had learned the skills of managing professionals only imperfectly. They could sometimes make her feel that the hostess herself was some kind of incompetent volunteer in an otherwise dependable performance. They would take correction from no one but Forbes, who paid the bill.

However modestly it had happened, Milly was glad to have the domestic reins back in her own hands where she had no sneaking suspicion that people had been hired to show her up in her own house. Red never did that. Every bit of her confidence came from Henrietta's teaching, and it came from doing the job well, not from knowing better than her betters. *How am I going to manage without her?*

Red knocked at the back door.

"Well!" Milly exclaimed. "Think of the devil!"

"I haven't come to apologize, Mrs. Forbes," Red said directly. "I've come to put away the vacuum cleaner and take down the living room curtains for the cleaner. I can put them in the trunk of your car. You'll be driving by Friday."

Milly stood meekly aside and let Red get on with her chores. In her invalid state, the house had seemed a kind of cocoon, and Milly hadn't minded the lack of light. Bonnie had been glad of any means to keep the old house warm. But now, as Red took down the drapes, the warm spring sun flooded into the house rich in recent memories of past summers when the family was together and Milly was willing slave to them all. She didn't have help except as the children

160

and Forbes could be coaxed into tasks unthinkable to ask of them in town.

"If I didn't have this great old barn of a house, I wouldn't need you," Milly said to Red's back.

"You love this place," Red said. "You wouldn't trade it even for Mrs. Hawkins'."

"For the water in Hen's well?"

"Not even for that," Red said, carrying the winter-dusty curtains out of the room.

Did she? Did she actually love this house? She would have thought she'd crabbed its charm right out of it in the cold and drafty winters, but, as the sun streamed in on the ample and amply used furniture, Milly knew Red was right. She had always loved not only the island but this house, for all her years of denying it. The house was generously shabby the way she imagined a country parsonage might be, and perhaps she could learn to live there like a parson's widow rather than the castoff wife of a man who could keep her a lot better than he was willing to.

The next time Red entered the house, she was suddenly right for the place though Milly doubted that she'd ever assume the appropriate shame at her condition. Well, Milly would have to strain to reach the piety of a parson's widow herself. Given the choice, she would rather be clean than moral. Red hadn't, after all, asked her to apologize either.

Red drove Karen's car onto the ferry as if she'd done it all her life, and Karen was not surprised. They'd practiced tight maneuvering for lack of high-speed roads and traffic. Karen had decided they

161

wouldn't go right into Victoria today. Instead they'd braid with the big road, ride a couple of exits, duck down into a suburb, try that traffic, and then go up onto the highway again. They would take time out for lunch and a bit of shopping, but their job for the day was driving. Since Red had passed her written test, she'd become impatient to try for her license.

"If we don't go pretty soon," Red said, "this baby's going to be driving the car."

Red still didn't look pregnant. In the warming weather she wore loose-fitting dresses as she always had. But she always looked now as if she'd just had a swim or a game of tennis or made love. And there was a washed clarity about her eyes. She wasn't even now pretty, but a young woman so distinctly alive might have caught a painter's eye.

Rather than sit in the coffee shop or one of the lounges, they walked the decks, the wind in their faces, the sun warm on their skin. Gulls alongside cruised at the speed of the ship or rested on the railings.

"They're flying most of the way," Karen said, "and we're walking."

"Are you tired?" Red asked. "We could sit down. It's just that I'm supposed to walk, and we'll be sitting most of the day."

"No," Karen said. "I like it better out of doors in this weather."

"I went back to Mrs. Forbes," Red said, not looking at Karen.

Karen stopped, and Red went on for a few steps before she realized she'd lost her companion. She turned around and gave Karen a tentative smile.

"Why did you do that?" Karen demanded.

Red shrugged.

"You don't need her money. I'm sure there are lots of other people you could work for."

"I'm used to it there," Red said, and, when Karen still looked disapproving, she added, "When I tried to think about telling Mrs. Hawkins, I couldn't."

"Hen doesn't have to be your conscience," Karen protested.

"She said to me once that Mrs. Forbes had been humiliated, and it took a long time to get over that."

"You don't get over it by humiliating other people!" Karen objected. "How long has it been since her husband had the good sense to leave her on the island?"

"Three or four years, I guess," Red said. "She has been a bit better lately since her operation and her daughter. And I told her I wouldn't apologize."

"*You* wouldn't? What about *her*?"

"That would be the day!" Red said laughing.

Red's company had become increasingly easy for Karen. She never felt she had to make conversation, nor did she have to censor what she thought even when Red might not agree. The only restriction Karen felt on the friendship was that they never simply met, without the excuse of driving lessons or dog-training sessions. Karen would have liked to ask Red over for supper, but, because Red knew she was gay, she might misinterpret the invitation. Red never suggested that Karen visit at her cabin. Karen doubted that she was ashamed of her place. Maybe she didn't want an invitation misunderstood either, or maybe it was more basic than that. Maybe the idea just didn't occur to her.

"Are you going to get a phone?" Karen asked.

"I've thought about it," Red said. "I've thought about how often people might phone me. Mrs. Forbes is always on the phone, and she doesn't have enough people to call."

"I suppose so," Karen said, seeing the point, "but it would be nice to get hold of you without sending out the army. And what about when the baby comes?"

"People have had kids miles from anywhere," Red said.

"Yeah," Karen said. "But they had to have a bunch in order for a few to survive."

"I don't think I want to have more than one," Red said. "This one wasn't all that easy to come by."

"Why did you pick Dickie?" Karen asked though Red had never spoken of him as the baby's father.

"I didn't think he'd care," Red said. "He wouldn't have, either. It's just that I got pregnant before he got bored."

"Did he know?"

"No," Red said. "I never wanted him to think it was any of his business."

Karen would have liked to ask other questions, but she was already afraid that Red felt pushed. Though Red's was an odd way to choose a father for her child, Karen did understand how Red had figured it out. Karen wondered if being a single parent would prove easier or more difficult now that Dickie was dead. If Dickie hadn't wanted to claim the child — and that was certainly likely — Sadie wouldn't have either. But, bereft of her only child, she might think differently about her claim to kinship.

As Karen had anticipated, Red was not intimidated by the speed of the big road. She liked it. Other cars

164

didn't distract her until she turned off the highway and drove around neighborhoods and commercial sections where traffic was less single-minded and pedestrians had the right-of-way. Red cursed at dogs and children so without reservation that it would have been hard to know she owned one and was expecting the other. She was sweating by the time Karen suggested they stop for lunch.

"It isn't driving that's the problem," Red said as they waited for their order. "It's trying to mind-read everything on legs or wheels."

"You're doing really well." Karen meant it, though her own nerves were also worn.

"Well," Red said, "I learned a long time ago everything's harder than it looks, even dusting, until you know how."

Red insisted on picking up the check. Karen made a polite protest. She liked Red's sense of responsibility and wondered if Hen had taught her that, too, or if it was something innate.

When they got back into the car, Karen noticed that Red's hands clutched the steering wheel even before she'd turned on the ignition.

"Ease up a bit," Karen said. "Or let me drive a bit?"

"No," Red said, letting go of the wheel and flexing her fingers several times. "I'm okay now."

Karen let her head for the big road and drive nearly into Victoria and back, the speed and ease gradually giving her back her confidence and pleasure.

"Maybe I should be a long-distance trucker," Red said. "It wouldn't be such a bad life for a kid."

"Most kids get carsick."

"How do you know things like that?" Red demanded.

"I went away to camp. Because I was an only child, my parents thought I needed extra practice getting along with kids my own age."

"Did you get along with them?"

"Well enough, I guess," Karen said. "But I never liked kids much. They were always being sick or mean."

"Not just kids," Red said. "People."

"Let's go back to Sidney now," Karen suggested. "I need to find a birthday present for my mother."

"Is it your mother or your father . . ." Red began a question she was obviously reluctant to finish.

"My father," Karen said. "You can tell by my last name, Tasuki."

"I can't," Red confessed. "I never know how Mrs. Forbes figures out who's Jewish or Hungarian or whatever by their last names. I don't have a last name. My mother called herself Smith. She said maybe I should be Heinz for fifty-seven varieties. She told people I was a little bit of everything bad: kike, wop, nigger, squaw."

"My father tells me I'm one hundred and fifty percent Canadian."

"Do they live in Vancouver?"

"No, my dad's in the East. My mother doesn't seem to live anywhere for very long."

They had taken the Sidney turn, and Karen was quiet now to let Red concentrate. When they got to the town center, Karen didn't insist that Red park on the street.

Red gratefully pulled into a parking lot. "I've had about enough of that for one day," she admitted.

"Do you want to wait in the car?"

"Maybe I will."

Karen was glad to be alone for a chore that baffled and would have embarrassed her had Red been with her. She had no idea of her mother's tastes. When she tried to think of colors her mother wore, Karen had no distinct memory. It would be easier to pick out something for Hen or Miss James or even the silly Milly Forbes. The few times she'd gone shopping with her mother, they'd looked for things for Karen which always hung in Karen's closet unworn. The presents her mother sent to her were tokens — bits of junk jewelry from around the world to go with a Christmas or birthday check drawn on an American bank account. Peggy had occasionally rummaged in Karen's drawer and found something that amused her; otherwise the gifts languished unused. Karen didn't wear jewelry. She supposed her gifts to her mother suffered a similar fate, knowledge which made her search the more futile. She went back to the car with a handbag, hoping her mother would like it only because Karen didn't.

Red was sound asleep. She looked even younger than her eighteen years, her soft mouth slightly parted, fine dark hair fallen over one eye. Karen wanted to reach out and brush the hair back off her face. It occurred to her for the first time that she would like to kiss that mouth. Stupid.

"Wake up," Karen said firmly, "and move over. I'm driving home."

"The doctor says there's nothing the matter with

167

you," Red said to Henrietta, who looked up at her from her bed.

"It isn't Thursday, is it?" Henrietta asked.

"People get up every day of the week," Red said, "even on a day when nobody is supposed to be cleaning the house."

"I was going to get up . . . later," Henrietta lied. "You mustn't bully me."

"A month is long enough," Red said.

A month? Had it really been a month? This limbo felt both like yesterday and the whole of her life. The difficulty wasn't that her bones ached so much; it was their weight she couldn't bear to haul around from room to room. Red and Karen had kept telling her she was losing weight but they didn't understand that her teeth were too heavy, her tongue was too large for her mouth, and she had to think to make herself swallow.

"Here's tea and juice," Red said. "Have that, and then I'll help you dress."

"I'll be just fine," Henrietta tried to assure her as she struggled to sit upright. "You just go along."

"Mrs. Hawkins," Red said, "I'm going to come here every morning and get you out of bed until you're back in the habit."

Henrietta hadn't the strength to protest that it was nobody's business whether she stayed in bed or not. She sat and sulked over her tray until Red came back into the room.

"Drink it," Red ordered, handing her the juice.

Henrietta accepted the glass reluctantly and took a small sip while Red watched her.

"It's fresh," Henrietta said, surprised by the sweetness and texture.

"The juice in the fridge is a week old. No wonder you don't want to drink it. How long is it since you went to the store?"

"Milly brought me some things the other day," Henrietta said.

"Ten days ago, and you told her not to call or come back till you called her. You haven't."

"She tires me, Red."

The mere thought of Milly made the juice glass in Henrietta's hand too heavy to hold.

"You could shop for yourself."

"You and Karen are always bringing me things. I don't seem to need all that much."

"When you get up, we'll go for a drive."

"I'm just not up to driving."

"I'll do the driving," Red said.

"You don't know how to drive," Henrietta said, relieved to remember the limit of Red's power.

"Yes, I do. Karen taught me, and I have my license."

"When did all this happen?" Henrietta asked, hating the little flash of fear that could invade her lethargy now and then.

"Over the past while. We're going to call on Miss James. She's better, but she still can't go out, and she's bored."

"I can't do that," Henrietta protested. "I don't have the voice for Miss James."

"She's expecting you," Red said.

"I'm not to be expected!" Henrietta replied crossly.

"Just let her talk," Red suggested, and grinned.

"What's so amusing?"

"I'm just glad to see you haven't forgotten how to be mad," Red said.

What Henrietta couldn't explain was that any emotion was a threat to her. Only by being still, by cultivating apathy, had she gradually been able to sink below the horror of Hart's death. If she let herself rise up again, it might be there waiting for her. Yet the burden her own body was becoming to her was not her will. It was beginning to suffer in a way she hadn't anticipated or intended. She needed Red's help to dress. And she needed Red's arm to lean on if she was going to try to walk to the car.

"I really can't do it," Henrietta said in some consternation as she sank into the passenger seat of her car. "I'm as weak as a kitten."

Blackie, held away by Red's order until Henrietta had sat down, now crowded into her knees.

"Blackie!" Red said firmly.

The dog cried but backed off, her tail wagging frantically.

"Shall I tie her up?" Red asked, "or can we take her along?"

"Take her," Henrietta said.

By the time Red had settled Blackie into the back seat, Henrietta had managed to swing her legs into the car. She closed her eyes and felt the sweet breath of the young dog at her ear.

"Blackie, sit!"

The dog sank back onto the floor behind their seats. Henrietta wondered vaguely at the confidence with which Red started the car and backed out of the garage. Earlier she might have felt a pang at someone else's taking on Red's education, but it was nothing but a relief to her now that Red had given herself over to another teacher. The movement of the car lulled her.

"Open your eyes!" Red ordered.

They were so heavy Henrietta wasn't sure she could. The reward, a view of her own fern- and fir-lined drive, was another small jolt of fear. The old fern fronds had not been cut back, and already the pale brown fists of new growth had begun to push their way through. She didn't want to risk even the ferns' need of her.

"I'll help you cut those back if you like," Red offered. "There's quite a bit around the place that needs doing."

Henrietta didn't answer. They were now out on the island road. Even here where she had no responsibilities, the living world seemed to clamor for her attention, from the pale greens of new growth on the evergreens to the blossoming berries. And there in a clearing by the side of the road were two does pausing to look before they bounded off into the bush.

As Red turned into Miss James' drive, Henrietta felt her bones settle. She was at the bottom of the sea.

"I truly can't," she managed to say.

"I know," Red said. "I'm just going to go in and tell her we'll come another day when you're stronger."

Henrietta didn't want strength, but she wanted to be free to choose against it. She was weighted here by her bones, really unable.

"Stay," Red said to Blackie.

The dog cried a little at Henrietta's ear before she settled back, resigned to her wait. And again

171

Henrietta closed her eyes against the sight of Miss James' wild little garden, beyond which the maples had leafed out to block her view of the sea. But she did remember that one day this would be Red's cottage, and she opened her eyes again because a child would one day play among these moss-covered rocks and scatterings of flowers.

Chapter XII

Karen's father had phoned from Vancouver and was arriving on the evening boat. She had swapped shifts with another ferry worker so that she could wait on the dock like any ordinary islander expecting company.

The dock was not as crowded as it would be in high summer, but the weather in late spring was already tempting visitors not tied to school schedules. The first vehicles off the ferry were campers inevitably driven by grey-haired or balding men whose wives sat beside them with laps full of knitting. Then came cars of young couples with one or two toddlers strapped into regulation car seats behind them. Very few people arrived alone unless they were islanders coming back from a day in town. And none of those wore a suit and tie and sat behind the wheel of an expensive rented car.

Karen swung into the seat beside her father quickly not to hold up the traffic. He glanced sideways at her, a look she returned only when his eyes had shifted back to the line of traffic. His extreme good looks always came as a shock to her. He had sent her a black-and-white photograph of himself, taken when he'd become president of his university, and in it his eyes were opened unnaturally wide, and his normally mobile mouth was clamped shut, macho Canadian through and through, no inscrutable Jap here. In person his skin was golden, his eyes dark honey and half-hidden, his mouth vulnerable to his moods.

"You look better," he said without glancing over at her again.

"I am," she answered.

The cottage did not please him but for the same reason Karen was beginning to grow impatient with it: there was neither room nor reason to make it her own.

"I have to move out for the month of August when the owners use it," she explained, "but that makes the rent very reasonable."

"Won't you have had enough of this life by then?" he asked.

"Of this cottage, maybe. I like the island."

"What exactly is it that you're doing?"

Karen didn't want to confess her jobs as a sin.

She didn't want the little confidence they had given her wiped out by the purse of her father's lips.

"I'm learning to live alone and take care of myself. I never have before."

"Does it suit you?"

She wanted to take a step back from him, away from his height of which he was so proud.

"It's beginning to," she said.

"You're a grown woman," he said, sighing as he sat down on the couch made suddenly more shabby as the setting for his expensive suit.

Karen did look carefully at him then because he was staring out at the view which was restless with water birds. She could not possibly be the cause of the strained sorrow in his face.

"Is anything wrong?" she asked.

"Your mother's dead," he said, still focused on the sea. "I've just come back from . . . I brought back a few of her things. I thought you might like . . . want . . ."

"When?"

"A week ago. She was always such a frail little thing."

"Of what?"

"Boredom? Terror? Exhaustion?"

"Those aren't things you die of," Karen said.

"Your mother killed herself."

All Karen heard in herself was *Might I?*

"I just sent her a handbag, for her birthday."

"I know," he said. "It was there. She hadn't opened it."

"I didn't mean anything to her," Karen said bleakly.

"Nobody did," her father said without comfort.

"Why not?"

"Maybe she just didn't have the energy."

They sat in awkward silence, Karen waiting to feel something out of which she might find something to say.

"We weren't divorced," her father said finally in a deliberate way. "She didn't want a divorce."

"Did you?"

"I haven't been celibate."

Why had he made it sound like a confession? Surely he didn't think she was unaware of his young women. He hadn't ever brought them home while Karen still lived there, but he made no secret of them.

"I've never thought she . . . was your fault."

"Did she?" he asked, offering another of his sideways glances.

"Oh, I don't know. We never talked about it. We never talked about anything."

"I married her because she reminded me of my mother," he said, and then he laughed.

Karen heard no bitterness in it, just a sense of the absurd. How could her tiny, blue-eyed mother remind him of his own? Karen had never met his mother. Both his parents had died in the camp. She assumed her mother's parents were either permanently estranged from their daughter or dead.

Her father stood again and turned to her, giving her the first direct look of his visit. He had never kissed her except with his eyes.

"I've eaten. Have you?"

"Yes," she said.

"Shall we take a look at this pub of yours?"

Karen had, ever since her mother had left them,

been both afraid for and proud of her father. Losing his wife, he seemed to have lost his ticket to the social world he was determined to feel comfortable in, and Karen was no help, both too young and not white enough. But tonight she could offer him the friendliness of her world.

Homer and Jane were just finishing a supper of fish and chips. Homer stood up to shake hands and say what a good job Karen did as a volunteer fireman, not back there at the hall making sandwiches but right out there with the men. Karen was embarrassed at what her father might think of such unladylike behavior, but she was also glad she'd found the courage to keep going to fire practices.

Adam, leaning on the bar with his beer, remembered the university her father was president of and asked respectful questions.

Only when Karen turned and saw Milly sitting alone with a glass of wine did she feel that old familiar panic of her younger years. Would Milly remember about the grave Karen had claimed was her great-grandfather's?

"Is that handsome man your father?" Milly called cheerfully.

He turned and smiled in return, never tired of the flattery of women, even women his own age, which Milly must be. And she was looking somehow softer tonight, her claws well hidden in her fur. Karen introduced them, but she steered her father firmly away and down into a lower, quieter nook of the pub before any conversation could develop.

"You have a lot of friends here," he observed when they'd given their orders.

"I work here most nights," Karen finally confessed, "and I work on the ferry dock, too."

"When you're not fighting fires?" he asked, raising his eyebrows.

"I've only been to one real fire. I nearly quit after that."

"You don't have to do this, you know," he said. "There's going to be money from your mother, and I'm not exactly hanging around waiting for government compensation. There's all the help in the world for you to *do* something with your life."

Karen shrugged.

"I want you to be all right," he said.

"Does it ever occur to you that I'd like to say that to you, too?" Karen asked.

"No," he answered, looking into his whiskey which was the same color as his eyes.

That would have been the moment for him to tell her he was going to marry again nearly at once, but he didn't. He wrote to her a week later.

Why hadn't he, who had some use for them, kept her mother's engagement and wedding rings? Karen put them, along with all the other jewelry her mother had sent, in the handbag he had also returned.

Karen grieved more for the robin that flew against her window than she did for her mother, and felt unnatural. Her only real emotion was the twinge of fear her blue eyes could give her as she glanced at herself in the mirror. *Could I?* She told no one of her mother's death, her father's remarriage. She thought of Dickie burning himself to death. She hadn't asked her father how her mother had done it. Now she never would.

* * * * *

Red put out a garden chair and helped Henrietta out to it where she could sit in the sun and teach Red what to do.

"I'm fine with vegetables," Red had confessed to her, "but I don't know a flower from a weed."

"You be careful with yourself now," Henrietta said.

"Women can just squat down and have their kids in the fields," Red said, herself squatting at the neglected ferns.

"Some may; most don't," Henrietta answered, flinching away from the memory of her own miscarriages.

She had no skin. Nearly everything touched some raw place. In that month of crazed apathy, she had not healed but had further damaged herself. Now she knew she had to eat. She had gradually to teach her neglected muscles to do her bidding. But what to do with the running sore of her psyche she didn't know.

Henrietta had not yet agreed to go out in the car again to call on Miss James. She still refused to see Milly. Even when the quiet Karen sometimes took Red's place, Henrietta felt at the edge of panic until she was alone again. A different sort of panic reasserted itself when she was alone, but at least then she was free to whimper, cry, talk to herself. Only Red's presence gave Henrietta some respite. Red was firm with Henrietta, but she didn't pry.

As Red's child grew, her own quietness had a different quality to it — not of griefs held back or needs not shared but of placid waiting.

"I'll plant bulbs at my place this fall," Red decided.

"Daffodils," Henrietta said. "The deer don't eat them."

Even that much advice cost effort, but it was possible. If she could keep up this slow pace of return, she might gradually be able to face the greater demands of life. *But how do you heal shame?*

"You don't. It heals itself," Red said.

"Are you reading my mind?" Henrietta demanded, the panic rising.

"Things that need to, come out," Red said quietly. "I thought maybe now you knew what they were."

"What things? What things?

"You haven't got anything to be ashamed of, Mrs. Hawkins. As you get better, you'll know that."

"How do you know that?" Henrietta demanded.

"I just know," Red said.

"You don't know anything! You're an ignorant child. Take me back to the house."

Henrietta trembled with the effort, and tears tracked down her face as unbidden and betraying as words. It didn't matter that Red beside her didn't look at her. Red knew.

"You're an indecent, ignorant girl!" Henrietta shouted from the safety of her kitchen chair.

Red looked at her for a speculative moment and then smiled. "I'll be back in a while."

It isn't funny! Had she spoken that aloud? Red had turned away and didn't answer. How could Henrietta have shouted at her like that? *I'm behaving like a Milly Forbes, spewing out my shame all over other people.* She hadn't even known she was doing it. *I can't trust myself.* She could not bear the idea of being no better than Milly, no better even than Sadie. At least Sadie had had the excuse of being drunk. Were all women, deserted, reduced to this? *I didn't even know I was.* But she hadn't really been alone in those years. She'd had the Hart that old man took to the grave with him. An illusion. That old man *was* Hart. But she couldn't have made all those visits if she had accepted that. That old man had been her duty, not her love. And what was the reward of all that duty but the shattering of illusion. *I am not a good woman. I didn't wake him because I didn't want to wake him. I didn't know he could kill Hart.*

Henrietta wanted to lie down. She didn't know if she had the strength to get to her bed, but she must. Slowly she worked her way from chair to doorjamb, from doorjamb to bookcase, from bookcase to bureau, her face soaked with tears, her nose running. Finally she stretched out on her bed. A cool breeze from the window gradually soothed her burning face, and she slept.

The dream was also gentle. Her husband's face, not so much as it had been before the strokes as beyond them, smiled at her. *I'm all right, Hen dear, I'm all right now.*

"So her ladyship's finally receiving guests, is she?" Milly asked.

"She's had a rough time, Mrs. Forbes," Red said.

"I thought she was made of tougher stuff."

"So did she."

"Well, I've missed her," Milly conceded. "I guess I'll just drop over there now and get out of your way.

What am I going to do, by the way, when that baby arrives?"

"Let the house get dirty for a week or two," Red answered.

"A *week* or two?"

"I can bring it with me, can't I?"

"Well, I suppose," Milly said. "I don't really mind babies until they learn to talk back."

Milly went into her bedroom to check her face. She hadn't been putting in much time on it lately. She looked older, and that somehow seemed appropriate, even a relief. Who was there to kid anyway? Tarting herself up for Hen wouldn't raise Hen's spirits. No woman felt better unless another was looking worse.

Milly was, however, shocked by Henrietta's appearance. She must have lost fifteen pounds, and she didn't have them to lose. Her clothes looked as if they belonged to someone else. And her beautiful hair had somehow simply wilted. She was an old, old woman.

"Hen!" Milly cried in distress. "What's happened to you?"

"I hardly know, Milly," Henrietta sighed. "But I think I'm over it. I just need time now to get my strength back. You're looking wonderful."

"Am I?" Milly asked, surprised.

"And after what you've been through!"

"It wasn't so bad," Milly admitted. "Except for getting tired awfully easily, I feel better than I have in years. I don't know why I waited so long. I want to go around recommending it to every woman I know."

Henrietta smiled her modifying smile and looked for a moment a bit more like herself.

"My daughter was awfully good to me, Hen. I'd forgotten how much I used to enjoy my kids. She works in a travel agency, you know, and she offered to send me off on a cruise."

"Where are you going to go?" Henrietta asked.

"Oh, nowhere," Milly said. "I haven't got the right clothes, and anyway I wouldn't want to travel around alone. Can you see me in a cathedral or a museum? The Grand Canyon would give me vertigo, and the one time I saw Niagara Falls, it was just noise. Do you know what Red said to me? She said, 'You love this house,' and the fact is, I do. I'm actually glad to be home."

"Red's had her hands full, hasn't she?" Henrietta said. "She's been here nearly every day."

"Not just her hands," Milly retorted. "What have you said to her about her condition?"

"Once I knew she wanted the baby, I told her I'd be any help I could."

"Oh, Henrietta Hawkins, have you no shame?" Milly mockingly demanded.

"Plenty," Henrietta answered, "but doesn't it seem funny now to think in terms like unwed mothers? Such a lot of bad sermons we were raised on."

"Aren't you even concerned it will be a bastard?"

"Heavens no," Henrietta replied. "That's just as silly."

"She says she's going to bring it to work. I don't know about you, but I don't have the money to pay her to baby-sit her own child."

"Maybe you'll have to do it then," Henrietta suggested.

"Are you going to suggest that to Miss James?"

"Ah, Miss James," Henrietta said thoughtfully. "I haven't seen her for weeks. She'll know by now, of course."

"It seems to me Red's expecting a good deal more tolerance than she has any right to," Milly said.

"Oh, she doesn't expect it," Henrietta said. "Why should she? She hardly knows what it is."

"And the father? Shouldn't he be made to take some responsibility? Disapproval isn't a sin, you know. It can nudge people in the right direction."

"I've never found that so," Henrietta replied.

Something in her tone reached and warned Milly not to press her any further. Milly's own energy for a good debate was also limited, and she had come close enough to losing Red to think it might not be such a bad idea to take a page out of Henrietta's book. The only disapproval that had done Milly any good was her own, and did she really enjoy it?

Chapter XIII

Karen was sitting on her deck, willing herself away from finding something to do. She needed to think about her mother. Each time she tried, she found she was thinking about herself instead. Karen had for a long time strained to identify not with her father exactly but with the Japanese side of herself. She didn't know why, since he had always been so firm in rejecting his own racial identity and had never offered her the slightest clue to its meaning. Aside from an occasional Japanese meal, there had never been anything in the house, a dish or a print, to suggest a Japanese heritage. It was as if her father had accepted the lessons of the camp or, to prove them wrong, insisted there was nothing different or distinctive about his race. Perhaps she clung to her difference to dissociate herself from a mother who had run away. Had Karen, too? Had she simply lacked the energy or insight or whatever it took to get through the difficulty with Peggy and come out on some better side? And, if she were like her mother, would she finally become so detached or frightened or despairing or whatever it was that she'd kill herself?

Karen had trouble remembering exactly what her mother looked like. When she took out the few photographs she had, it was the photographs rather than her mother that were familiar to her. How could she grieve for someone she didn't even clearly remember? Peggy had never understood why Karen didn't resent her mother. But her mother had never been very clear to her even when they had lived in the same house. Whatever sense Karen had of her had faded gradually. The woman she occasionally went to visit was a stranger who had wanted to please her but didn't know how. What they had shared was embarrassment. And perhaps regret, though that was a stronger and more lasting emotion than Karen could really claim.

"I'm sorry, Mother," Karen said aloud and did not know what she meant by it.

Behind her in the cottage, the phone rang.

"I've got a phone," Red announced.

"What made you finally decide?" Karen asked.

"The baby, I guess. And Mrs. Hawkins and Miss James. I haven't given Mrs. Forbes the number."

"All she has to do is look it up."

"Not for a while."

"Listen," Karen said. "Why don't I make up some sandwiches and we can go up on the bluff for lunch?"

Red hesitated and then said, "Okay."

Since the driving lessons were over, Karen had seen very little of Red, and she missed her. Without being able to phone, she'd had no casual way of reconnecting; for Red, aside from being busy with her ailing old women, was never just out and about these days. Karen knew the whole island was speculating now about whose baby Red was carrying, though such conversations ceased abruptly at Karen's approach. Rat was the only one of the young men to have a good word to say about Red. He was grateful for a free baby sitter so that he and his wife could occasionally come to the pub together. It was he who had asked Karen whose kid it was. "Ask her," Karen replied. Rat had shrugged, obviously embarrassed.

On the bluff at lunch time, they might meet an early tourist or two or a local walking a dog, but they wouldn't have to deal with the rude stares Red had encountered from the young men even before her pregnancy was obvious. Karen couldn't decide whether Dickie's being the father would make Red better or worse in their eyes.

"I've missed you," Karen said as Red and Blackie got into the car.

"It's just this week Mrs. Hawkins has started to drive again," Red said.

"She's really better?"

"Getting there."

"And Miss James?"

"Fed up she isn't dead."

Karen laughed.

"She doesn't think it's decent for someone her age to live through pneumonia."

As Karen turned up the road to the bluff, they fell silent. It was no more than a dirt track which took them up into the deep woods, cool on the warmest day of summer, sometimes impassable in winter when its deep potholes were filled with water, the ditches overflowing. The car lumbered along like a clumsy tank, and Karen wished they were walking instead, part of the silence around them. Emily Carr's woods these were, and Karen had known them first in her paintings in the Vancouver Art Gallery. Emily Carr had probably wanted to be an Indian, the way she ventured into the forests and sought out the great totems. Maybe everyone here was a displaced person. You would be even if you were an Indian.

"Do you ever feel like a displaced person?" Karen asked.

"You'd have to have a place to come from to feel like that," Red said.

"Nobody really comes from here," Karen said.

"Dickie did," Red said. "I can tell my kid his father and his grandfather both came from here."

Was Red assuming she'd have a boy? Did she want a boy? Karen hesitated to ask such a question. She didn't want to sound like a lesbian separatist, even though she couldn't imagine why anyone would want a boy. They grew up too alien and hard-surfaced.

They got out of the car and Red stopped to put Blackie on a leash. By now the dog came obediently when called but Blackie still couldn't resist a flushed deer, and she was young enough to be careless of her way on paths dangerously close to the cliff edge.

Karen couldn't wait. She strode over to the side of the rough parking lot and looked out over the pass, across to the clusters of other islands. Today it was clear enough to see the snow-defined Olympic range in the States. When Red and Blackie came up beside her, she turned to the path that led them to a high meadow where they could have their lunch. All along their way, tiny lavender and yellow and white wild-flowers poked up among the grasses.

"I never learn their names," Karen said.

"Miss James says names aren't any use because you just forget them. The only thing worth remembering is poetry."

"Do you ever read poetry?" Karen asked.

"She teaches me. I memorize poems for her."

"I don't think I've read a poem since I left school," Karen said.

"Kids like poems," Red said.

"I'll get the baby a book of poems, shall I?" Karen suggested.

"If you can find one at the thrift shop."

"Oh Red, we don't always have to be so spartan."

Karen spread a beach towel a few yards away from the cliff edge so that their view, when they sat down, was mostly sky, alive with gulls at eye level, an occasional plane high above on its way to or from Alaska. In the middle air the sun caught the white of the heads and tails of coasting eagles.

Red lay on her back looking up, her mound of belly like a little hill. As she watched, she began to recite:

"If you would keep your soul
From spotted sight or sound,
Live like a velvet mole;
Go burrow underground."

"That's a bit grim, isn't it?" Karen asked, suddenly very aware that Red carried a dead man's child without remorse.

"I make a better mole than an eagle," Red said, grinning. "Ah, see him kick!"

Karen could see the jumping flesh of Red's stomach, little mole inside his hill.

"Put your hand just there," Red said.

Karen hesitated, but the invitation was so impersonal that she reached out and laid her hand on Red, feeling the force of that tiny life beneath the thin layers of cloth and skin.

Below them a ferry sounded at the west entrance of the pass.

"Do you ever think about your mother?" Karen asked.

"Not much," Red said. "I don't buy her birthday presents."

Karen pictured the ugly handbag, heavy with useless jewelry.

"Well, I do think about her more now," Red admitted. "She was only fourteen when I was born."

"Where is she now?"

"In jail. She killed a man," Red answered flatly.

"Oh Red!" Karen cried.

"She wanted me to say she did it to protect me, and I wouldn't do it," Red said. "I ran away."

"How old were you?"

"Fourteen," Red said.

"Why did she do it?" Karen asked.

"Because she felt like it, I guess," Red said. "I used to dream about it and worry about it at first. I don't any more. I can just remember *her* sometimes now. But in my head my mother's dead."

"Mine is, too," Karen said, admitting and not admitting, not sure why killing yourself seemed more shameful than murder.

"There are choices," Red said, sitting up. "Anybody can make choices."

Karen did not feel that confident. Struggling against her passivity, she had been trying to make choices, but she wasn't at all sure they were the right ones. In Red's circumstance she would have been suicidal, if not from the terror of giving birth and taking total responsibility for another human being, then from the disapproval and hostility that surrounded Red. Karen could not have ignored it.

"Eat?" Red asked.

"Of course," Karen said, getting out the sandwiches. "I even remembered Blackie."

She tossed a couple of biscuits to the young but increasingly patient dog. "You've done a good job with her," Karen said.

Red smiled and reached out to her dog. It was her own confidence she was building for the more important and complex business of raising a child, and Karen envied that sense of purpose in Red. She wondered if she would have to live her own life without it.

* * * * *

Henrietta was still a bit shaky, but she had put off her visit to Miss James long enough. They'd had several conversations on the phone, and though Miss James made no demands, Henrietta knew she was still housebound and lonely.

"Oh, Hen, I have missed you," the old woman confessed.

Henrietta was as tactful as Miss James, not mentioning the change for the worse in each of them. In each setback now, there was some permanent damage. Miss James' skull glowed through her nearly transparent skin.

"I don't know which has been more distressing, your being sick or my being alive."

It surprised Henrietta to realize she herself had never wished to die, even through the worst of it.

"I can't just wander off like an old Eskimo, not in early June, but what is that child going to do if I'm not dead by August?"

"She'll manage perfectly well," Henrietta replied.

"Will she?" Miss James demanded. "It's a very willful thing she's doing. I said to her, 'You do know they grow up and leave home, don't you?' "

"There's satisfaction in that, you know," Henrietta said.

"And what's Sadie making of it, do you know?"

"I haven't seen Sadie in months," Henrietta admitted.

"Red refuses to talk about the father. She's behaving as if it's going to be a virgin birth."

"Would Dickie have had anything to do with it if he'd lived?"

Miss James sighed. "I have too much time to think, when the only useful thing I could possibly do is die. I wondered for a while if I was making a mistake, leaving the house to her, thinking after all she didn't have the gumption to live alone. She doesn't think it's gumption, mind you. But, of course, she'll need the house all the more when the child comes. But will she want it?

"I've been reading Emily Dickinson, a mistake at my age, I think. She's very unsettling."

Miss James reached over for a book on the table by her chair.

"Listen to this:

> I had been hungry all the years;
> My noon had come to dine;
> I, trembling, drew the table near,
> And touched the curious wine.
>
> 'Twas this on tables I had seen,
> When turning, hungry, lone,
> I looked in windows, for the wealth
> I could not hope to own.
>
> I did not know the ample bread;
> 'Twas so unlike the crumb
> The birds and I had often shared
> In Nature's dining room.
>
> The plenty hurt me, 'twas so new,
> Myself felt ill and odd
> As berry of the mountain bush
> Transplanted to the road.

Nor was I hungry; so I found
That hunger was a way
Of persons outside windows,
The entering takes away."

Though Miss James' voice was loud and flat, she brought such intent intelligence to the poem that Henrietta was moved by it, and yes, unsettled.

"I was proud of being disinherited," Miss James said. "I don't want to hurt her pride. It's about all she's got."

"I don't see why it wouldn't make her proud," Henrietta said, but she felt uncertain, human emotions being darker and more complex than she had realized until recently.

"It's for me after all," Miss James concluded. "A last little vanity of having something to leave behind. I want her to be grateful to me."

"That's nothing to be ashamed of," Henrietta protested.

"Isn't it?"

"Don't change your will," Henrietta said, surprised at her own firmness.

"No, I don't suppose I will," Miss James said, smiling. "I've been hermit-hearted enough."

Moving with careful slowness through Miss James' garden, Henrietta wondered at that long life of proud solitude, cut off from family, without close ties of any sort. Had there been lovers, beloved friends somewhere along the way, left behind or outlived? Henrietta doubted it somehow. If Miss James had experienced ordinary attachments through her life, surely she wouldn't be as fastidious about her motives as she was now. Or perhaps that was simply

194

one of the hazards of old age, a filling up of empty hours with over-elaborate doubts and judgments, an idle trying on of one moral hat after another. Maybe poetry wasn't good for people over a certain age, a certain kind of it anyway. Better to take up solitaire or crossword puzzles.

Henrietta smiled at the first bloom in a patch of lilies and wondered if any of her own were out. She wanted enough strength back to garden again. Red was learning quickly, but the look of the garden was only half the pleasure. She wanted the feel of the earth in her hands again, the sense of accomplishment.

At home, though her first outing had tired her, Henrietta walked slowly about her land, calling on her flowers. Hart's roses needed feeding.

As Milly entered the pub, she noticed with distaste that Sadie was cackling drunk among a circle of young men willing to ply her with gin and then drive her home. Milly flinched at the memory of driving Sadie home after Dickie's funeral. Dickie. Dickie was the father! Why hadn't something that obvious occurred to her before?

Milly sat down to that revelation and checked it out mathematically, counting back the months on her fingers. Then she recalled Red the morning after the fire. She hadn't been vomiting up grief or remorse; she'd been pregnant. And even before Dickie died, Red hadn't intended to make him marry her. She'd already dropped him. She hadn't ever wanted Dickie — she'd wanted a child. Such casual use of a man shocked Milly far more than the casual use Dickie had obviously made of Red, mindless of the consequences. But would he have, if he'd known? He'd already built himself a house. Women weren't the only nest builders. Forbes hadn't been a diaper changer the way young men were now, but he'd loved his children. Dickie might have loved his. Red hadn't even gone to the funeral. Like a mating spider she was without an ounce of human feeling. She didn't even have the decency to feel ashamed.

"Are you ready to order?" Karen asked.

"It's Dickie's child!" Milly announced in triumph.

Sadie sailed a laugh out over all the company.

"You're going to be a grandmother," Milly called over to her.

"Serves her right," Sadie said in satisfaction. "Got the last laugh after all, he did."

Karen had turned away and was disappearing into the kitchen.

"Hey!" Milly called after her. "I want to order."

Who was Karen to take offense over the facts of life?

"I'll take your order," the bartender offered.

"What's with Miss Half-Jap? Too good for her job, is she?"

"Red's a friend of hers," the bartender excused gently.

"She cleans for me," Milly said, "and I've been kind enough to let her keep her job."

"What will you have?"

"The chowder and a half liter of white wine."

The young men at Sadie's table had closed in around her, and, before Milly's supper arrived, they were walking Sadie to the door. She hesitated by Milly's table.

"It'll be none of mine," Sadie said to Milly.

"Come on, Sadie," one of the young men urged. "Time to go."

"But what have you to be so high and mighty about?" Sadie demanded. "Some of us can't catch a man. Some of us can't keep one."

"Oh, go throw up some place else," Milly said in disgust.

She turned away from Sadie and met Karen's peculiar blue gaze as she stood waiting to serve Milly.

She ate without appetite, troubled not so much by Sadie's drunken attempt to put her down as by a new weariness of spirit. She no longer had the energy to enjoy her own spite. She was still convalescent and needed to cosset herself.

"Dessert?" Karen asked.

Milly had lately been indulging in desserts.

"Not tonight," Milly said, and then added, "Your father's a very handsome man. You look a bit like him."

She had meant to say something to indicate how watered down those pure good looks were in Karen's half-breed face, but she didn't. She was exhausted.

Chapter XIV

Karen was helping Rat coil the hoses at the end of fire practice when Red's call came into the hall.

"She says there's no hurry," Homer reported. "Old Miss James is dead."

"On a day like this?" Rat asked, dropping his piece of hose.

The July sun shone down on their vigorous, contented bodies as they stood together with nothing to make of the news.

"Somebody ought to get to Red right away," Karen decided. "I'll go."

"I'll come with you," Rat offered.

"I'll be along as soon as we finish up here," Homer said.

Red was sitting outside on the steps of Miss James' cottage when they arrived. Karen could tell she had been crying.

"Where is she?" Rat asked.

"In her chair by the window," Red said.

"Homer's coming right along," Rat said over his shoulder as he went inside.

"It's what she wanted," Karen said, sitting down beside Red on the steps.

"I know," Red said, "but I didn't. I wanted her to see the baby. It's not long now. She could have waited for that."

"Is there anyone to notify?" Karen asked.

Red shook her head.

"Hen?" Karen suggested.

Red shrugged.

"Oh Red," Karen said, putting an arm around her oddly insubstantial shoulders.

"I've never seen anyone dead like that," Red said. "Just dead. Nothing else but dead."

"I'm sorry you had to find her," Karen said.

"Who else?" Red asked.

"Do you feel all right?"

"I guess so," Red said, touching her stomach.

Karen took her arm away quickly as she heard Rat coming back.

He stood on the step above them, looking down the drive for the ambulance Homer would be driving.

"Do we know what to do?" he asked.

"She said she left instructions in the middle

drawer of her desk," Red said. "She belongs to the Memorial Society."

"That simplifies things," Rat said, approving. "Who's next of kin?"

"Nobody," Red said.

"Did she have a lawyer?"

"In town," Red answered.

The ambulance swung into the drive, and Homer got out. He looked around at the brightly blooming garden and shook his head. Then he looked down at Red.

"You all right, girl?"

She nodded without looking up at him.

"You got a bag with you?" Rat asked.

Homer nodded and turned back to the ambulance.

"Thing about a body," Rat said, addressing his remark to no one in particular, "it's just a body."

Karen wondered if she would feel that way. She had no interest in finding out. She urged Red off the steps and out of the way as the two men went back into the house.

"We don't have to watch," Karen said.

"I do," Red answered.

So Karen stood with her a little distance off among Miss James' flowers, until Rat and Homer carried out the bag which contained the body. When they'd placed it in the ambulance, Homer walked back to the young women.

"We ought to lock this place up," he said.

"There's no key," Red said. "She didn't believe in that."

"Well, there's all her things," Homer said, looking worried. "People hear she's gone, they might . . ."

"Shouldn't we call Hen?" Karen suggested again. "She'd probably know what to do."

"Miss James didn't want a funeral," Red said, "or anything."

Homer was looking at the door.

"I could get a padlock," he decided. "Could you maybe just stay here until I send somebody to fix it?"

Red nodded.

"I can, too," Karen declared. "And I'm going to phone Hen."

"Tell her we're getting hold of the Memorial Society. We'll take care of that," Homer said and then turned to Red. "I'm real sorry, Red. You should be looking out for yourself now."

Rat came up beside Homer.

"Come have supper with us tonight," he said to Red.

"Thanks," Red said.

Karen felt a flash of frustrated resentment. Why should Rat be able to be so casual in offering comfort when Karen hadn't ever dared to ask Red for a meal because of what Red might think, what other people might think? Then she was ashamed of resenting any small kindness that came Red's way.

"Do you want to stay out here while I phone?" Karen asked.

"No," Red said. "I'll come with you."

How cheerful the kitchen was, full of late-afternoon sun. This house was so much Miss James' that its mood should have shifted into mourning. But there on the counter was a half-eaten jar of blackberry jelly, a banana and an apple in a pretty pale blue bowl, and fresh daisies on the table.

Red sat down at it and put her head on her arms. Karen moved to the phone, noticing the volume adjuster. Henrietta's hello boomed out at her.

"It's Karen," she said. "I'm over at Miss James' with Red. I'm sorry to have to tell you Miss James is dead. Homer and Rat have taken her away, and they're going to get in touch with the Memorial Society, and Homer's going to get a lock for the door. We're not sure what else we should do."

Karen talked so quickly she didn't give Henrietta time to respond. She felt clumsy and stupid. When she hung up, she turned to Red's bowed head and said, "She's coming right over."

Red sat up and rubbed her eyes. Karen went into Miss James' bathroom and found a washcloth. She dampened it and went back to Red who offered up her face to that soothing like a small child.

Henrietta sat for a moment to take in what Karen had said. She was surprised to find how calm she was, and grateful. At times in the last weeks she had despaired of ever asking anything of herself again. For someone so emotionally dependable for so many years, it was a humiliation to be unable to trust her own responses, little shreds of hysteria floating up at her at the oddest moments.

Lily Anne James was dead, as she wished to be, in time for Red's baby to have a home. It seemed to Henrietta quite an accomplishment to die on such a calm, bright summer day. Though she would miss Miss James, it was not going to be a hard mourning. There was to be no funeral, but there would have to be something for those who needed it. They were all too interdependent to do without.

In the meantime, she must go over to the house and tell Red what Miss James' will contained. Perhaps she should take it out first and read it to be sure that some ancient quirk of scruple hadn't made Miss James change it at the last moment.

Henrietta found Red and Karen sitting at the kitchen table drinking tea out of Miss James' fine china cups. One had been set out for her.

"Thank you for coming," Karen said, getting up to offer Henrietta a chair. "I'm sorry I babbled like that on the phone."

"It's always a shock," Henrietta said, giving Karen a reassuring pat on the arm. "Red, you mustn't mind too much, dear. She wanted to go."

Red nodded bleakly. The strength of her loyalty to Miss James had been no less than to Henrietta in these last hard months. Even a desired death could be no comfort to her.

"It's funny to think she had no family," Karen said, "no one at all to notify."

"We're her family," Red said.

"Yes, we are," Henrietta agreed. "That's how she felt about it exactly."

Henrietta took her time over tea, mixing what she now recognized as platitudes with their musings. But platitudes were the sane safeties necessary to cover up feelings too dangerous to deal with if they could be avoided.

"You mustn't upset yourself too much," Henrietta said to Red who had begun to cry again. "You have to think of the baby."

It was time to check the will and to offer Red the

solider evidence that Miss James really did think of Red as her own. The will was in the desk drawer she had taken it from to show Henrietta, and it said what Henrietta had expected it to. She sighed in satisfaction. It wasn't often solutions were so clearly satisfactory. Now Red could move out of that little cabin with its dangerous wood stove and have her baby here in a house she already knew how to care for, with all Miss James' books, with her fine china.

"No!" Red cried out. "No!"

Nothing either Karen or Henrietta could say did anything to quiet her.

"How could she want to die for the baby?" Red wailed.

"This isn't the way to think about it," Henrietta protested.

She might have been watching herself, engulfed in guilt and shame and anger she could hardly explain to herself now.

"Listen to me, Red," she said firmly. "Listen to me. You mustn't do this. You haven't got time for it. You're about to be a mother."

"I don't want the baby!" Red shouted. "I don't!"

She ran out of the house she had just been told was hers. Karen followed her.

Henrietta sat down heavily. She hadn't the strength to go after them. It was the first violent shaking of grief, that was all. It wasn't a mistake. It couldn't be.

Karen followed Red running clumsily down the path to the shore. When Karen was only a few yards from her, Red suddenly stopped, put her hands on her stomach, and looked down at her feet.

"It's broken," she said softly, watching the water of her womb flood down her legs into her shoes.

"I'll call the ambulance," Karen said. "Come on. Come on back up to the house."

"The ambulance is gone," Red said.

Karen then remembered it would be on the evening ferry taking Miss James' body away to be cremated.

"We'll call the helicopter. Come on."

"No," Red said. "Take me home."

"You can't go home," Karen said.

"Yes I can."

Red was in so irrational a state that Karen was afraid to do anything to cross her. She might throw herself into the sea. Karen could take her home and phone from there.

Red allowed herself to be led back to Karen's car. Karen was afraid to leave her even long enough to tell Henrietta what had happened. When Henrietta heard the car, she'd know Karen had Red with her.

At the cabin, Blackie, tied to a stump, barked and wagged her tail.

"Lie down!" Red commanded, and then she turned back to Karen and said, "I don't need any help."

"Of course you do," Karen said.

"I can do it myself."

"You can't be alone. What if something went wrong?"

"It's all wrong," Red said flatly.

"It isn't!" Karen said, and she was suddenly more angry than frightened. "Miss James would be ashamed of you, behaving in this stupid, ungrateful way. She thought you had guts. She thought you could cope. She thought —"

"Well, she's right. I can," Red said between her teeth. "So get out."

"I won't," Karen said. "I won't leave you. I don't know the first thing about having a baby. I don't even know how to boil water on a wood stove, and I'll probably throw up or faint. But I'm not leaving you alone."

Red turned away to the neatly made bed in the corner of her one-room cabin, stretched out on it and put an arm across her eyes.

For the first time Karen had a chance to look around an interior she had often imagined. It was very plain and neat but even more primitive than she had expected. There was no electricity, no running water. A couple of kerosene lamps and several candles were all the light they would have as night came on. If she was to boil water, she'd not only have to build a fire in the wood stove but haul water from the well. How had Red ever imagined she could take care of a baby here? But obviously she had. At the foot of her bed was an old-fashioned cradle, beside the one window an old wooden rocking chair. Two straight chairs drawn up to a bare table were all the other furniture Red had. Her clothes hung on a few pegs in the wall in one corner of the room. There were a dozen books on a shelf under the window, the thickest one on childbirth. Karen reached for it, opened its densely printed pages and threw it down again.

On the bed Red's arm was now over her mouth, and her eyes were hard and staring.

"Red," Karen said, going to her and kneeling by the side of the bed, "I've got to get help."

"Call Jane," Red said with an effort.

"Jane?"

Red nodded.

Why Jane? Was she a midwife? Well, whatever she was, at least she was somebody else, and anybody else would be better equipped than herself. At least Jane had had children of her own. Karen looked up her number, thanking heaven for the phone.

"The car's down at the fire hall," Jane said. "Homer left it there when he took the ambulance."

"Can you get somebody to bring you? I don't want to leave her."

"I'll get there," Jane said.

"Thank you," Karen said. "Thank you very much."

Red was resting easier. Karen moved one of the straight chairs over to the bed, sat down and took Red's hand.

"How far apart are they?" Karen asked, a question that came out of TV shows rather than any knowledge.

"Two or so minutes."

"Does that mean it'll be pretty soon?"

Red's hand closed down on hers, and Karen held her breath. When Red's hand relaxed, Karen blacked out for a second. What was she doing, holding her breath like that?

"I think so," Red said in answer to a question Karen couldn't remember asking.

Through the next pain, Karen nearly hyperventilated. She had no idea what Red was supposed to do. She only hoped Red remembered what she had read and was doing it right. Karen looked at the book she had thrown on the floor and wondered at how much womanly knowledge she had refused to learn.

"I'm sorry," she said and knew it was what she always said.

Though the sky still held some high summer light, it was nearly dark in the cabin. She had lighted a couple of candles. She had found a towel to wipe sweat from Red's face. And she struggled against willing Red to wait, wait until there was help.

Finally Jane was there, remarkably calm and knowledgeable and blessedly bossy, quite unlike the timid little woman Karen saw at the pub with Homer. Karen was actually hauling in water, building a fire in the stove, lighting the lamps, all under Jane's clear direction while Jane also directed Red whose concentration was entirely focused now. She never cried out, but she grunted harshly, more like a man pitting his whole strength against a stubborn object.

There was a wet sound, and then the room was flooded with a new fleshly smell. The object in Jane's hands mewed rather than cried, and Jane gave a low laugh.

"It's a girl, Red," she said.

"Oh, the poor little thing," Red said, "the poor little thing," and reached out her arms.

Karen stood back, tears of relief bathing her face. A girl, poor little thing indeed, but a girl.

"What are you going to name her?" Jane asked.

"Blue."

Karen's tears turned to laughter. It was so like Red. She hadn't thought of a blue-eyed child. She was naming the baby for herself.

* * * * *

"Blue! What kind of a name is that!" Milly
demanded.

"I think it comes out of an old cowboy song,"
Henrietta said, "but I'm not sure."

"The least you'd think she could do was give the
poor child a decent name," Milly said.

"I don't know," Henrietta said. "It's not as silly
as Hen."

"Well, but you have a *real* name."

They were sitting out on Milly's deck, having
morning coffee on another lovely summer day.

"What's important is that they're both all right,"
Henrietta said. "It was awfully hard on her finding
Miss James like that."

"Is it true what I hear, that Miss James has left
her her house?"

Henrietta nodded.

"Why doesn't she name her for Miss James,
then?"

"Lily Anne?" Henrietta asked.

"Well . . . I must say she seems to land on her
feet, with all her sins rewarded."

"It's a sweet cradle you've given her," Henrietta
said.

"The baby had to have somewhere to sleep, and I
don't suppose Miss James had one of those tucked up
in *her* attic."

Milly did feel outclassed by Miss James' gesture.
She'd been so rarely generous in these last years that
she resented having her sense of beneficence cut
short. She was also irritated that Henrietta had seen
the baby, and she had not. But some scruple she

209

didn't understand in herself was making her wait for an invitation which probably would not be forthcoming. She would have to wait until Red came back to work.

"Red was very pleased. She said she liked having something with a history for the baby."

"I've got an old highchair up there, too," Milly said. "She can have that when she needs it. Why I've kept those things around all these years I can't think."

"For grandchildren?"

"Having children seems the farthest thing from my kids' minds. It's gone out of fashion in their generation."

"Some of them are waiting longer, and that's not a bad thing," Henrietta replied.

Henrietta was born to be resigned, Milly thought, and was not sorry to see her looking around for her handbag. She'd gone a bit dithery since she'd been sick. Without Hart, she didn't seem to have reason enough to pull herself back together.

"Do you think we ought to do something about Miss James?" Henrietta asked as she got up to go. "Just a little tea or something like that?"

"Who'd go?" Milly asked.

"Probably most people," Henrietta said, but there was no energy in her voice.

"It's not necessary, Hen," Milly said.

"Perhaps not," Henrietta said. "It does seem sad, though, just to go."

When Henrietta had taken herself off, Milly remained sitting in the sun, aware that her own sense of importance had begun to fade, that it was harder for her to imagine being the cause for concern for her children. When a child you had born and raised could simply disappear, be unheard of for years, you could almost hope something dreadful had happened to her to cancel the sense of her complete indifference. Milly had bought that cradle for Nora, who might even have children of her own by now. Odd. Had she and Forbes really been that dreadful? The other two seemed to have managed, but they'd been younger. Nora. Milly thought of her as a baby or with a baby, the two images blurring. She wanted to see Red's baby. She wanted to be asked.

Chapter XV

Henrietta rummaged around in her own store of goods, looking for something for Red's baby. Even as she looked, she knew she wouldn't find anything. Having lost so many babies, she had become superstitious about things accumulated for them. She only remembered now how she had given away everything, had not even so much as a diaper waiting for the child who finally lived, and she'd given away each of her sons' clothes and toys as he had outgrown them. How long it had taken her, out of what abundance of sorrow, to see that she couldn't outwit the jealous gods. They took whom they pleased. She had that cumbersome silver tea set, all that china, but there wasn't so much as a baby cup or spoon to hand on to the grandchildren she had resolutely refused to hope for.

Then she found a lambskin still sealed in cellophane, a spare she had kept for Hart when the one he had been using became worn past comfort. He had been removed from her care before he needed it. Under it she found still unused very soft towels also intended for Hart. Needs of the newborn and the dying were often similar. The feel of that softness returned her to a self who had not seemed to mind the tending of either helpless child or helpless man.

With these excuses to visit Red again, so soon after her first quick call to assure herself that Red and the baby were all right, Henrietta set out. She hoped, once the presents were offered and she'd chatted with Red awhile, that it might be possible to raise the problem of Miss James' house. Henrietta had talked with the lawyer. Though it would take some time to settle the estate, there was no reason why Red couldn't move in at once. But Henrietta would have to be cautious.

She found Red sitting up in the rocker nursing the baby. The table was cluttered with baby things, boxes of Pampers, stuffed animals.

"People keep coming by," Red said in puzzled explanation.

"Well, of course," Henrietta said, not as confident of this community response as she sounded.

"I haven't even had time to put anything away," Red apologized. "There really isn't any place to put it."

"Well, this can go into the cradle," Henrietta said, taking the wrapper from the lambskin. "And you can take it wherever you take the baby so that she'll feel at home."

"It's beautiful," Red said, reaching out to touch it.

The baby, distracted, began to fuss.

"We shouldn't talk while you're nursing," Henrietta said. "Shall I make a pot of tea?"

"I'm out of water. You'd have to go to the well."

Henrietta was glad of a chore that would leave Red quiet with the baby. As she worked the pump, she admitted a primitive pleasure in standing out in the carefully tended little vegetable garden. But it was one thing to experience this old-fashioned ritual in the warm summer sun, another in the cold of winter. Red knew that. She'd lived here for four years, but not with a baby. Surely she'd see the reason for moving to Miss James' house. Carrying the bucket back, Henrietta saw Blackie's rope attached to a stump.

"Where's the dog?" she asked.

"Karen's taken her for a run," Red said, holding the baby on her shoulder. "She doesn't want her to get jealous of the baby, but she won't. She already understands about Blue. Better than Karen does."

Henrietta admired how relaxed and confident Red was with the baby. It had been an easy birth, Jane had said, hardly any tearing. It was those wonderful wide hips. So little had been given to Red, Henrietta felt gratitude that at least the shape of her body was a blessing.

"Do you want to hold her?" Red offered.

"Oh yes," Henrietta said, reaching out for her, a

good-sized baby for only two days old, but, of course, tiny. "How much does she weigh?"

"About eight pounds, we figure," Red said. "A roasting chicken."

Henrietta wanted to suggest having her checked by a doctor, but Jane had warned her not to push Red about such things. She wouldn't be irresponsible, but she wanted as little help as possible. Blue was a healthy baby.

"Little Blue," Henrietta said, smiling down at the tiny face which rewarded her with a large yawn.

"Why not let her try the lambskin?" Red suggested.

The baby settled at once. The kettle whistled on the wood stove. The sound made Henrietta aware of how warm she was, for, even with the door and window open, the stove threw off too much heat.

"We could take chairs outside," Red suggested.

They were still sitting in the doorway when Karen and Blackie returned.

"She'd play fetch all day if you let her," Karen said. "Shall I tie her up?"

"No," Red said. "She's all right."

Red let the dog push past her into the cabin where she went right up to the cradle, nosing the lambskin and the baby.

"Is that all right?" Karen asked nervously.

"She can't learn to baby-sit without smelling her," Red said.

Satisfied, Blackie backed away, snorted, and lay down a few feet from the cradle.

"I was wondering," Red said, turning to Henrietta, "if it would be all right if Karen rented Miss James' place for August."

Karen gave Henrietta a nervous glance.

"Well, Red, it's yours," Henrietta said. "The lawyer says you can move in yourself whenever you want."

"Then she can," Red said.

"But only if you —" Karen began.

"I can't now," Red said. "I had this all figured out here, and I just can't think about anything else yet."

"It would be so much more convenient —" Henrietta began.

"I'm used to this," Red said firmly, but then she added, "Maybe later, maybe in September."

Henrietta would have to be content with that for now.

When she left, Karen walked back up the road with her.

"I didn't want to agree to it," Karen said. "I tried to persuade her, but she somehow needs to prove something about doing it her way. And maybe she needs time, too, before she'd feel comfortable there. I didn't ever go in after Miss James died, but it's a bit hard, even for me."

"But she is over . . . hating the idea?" Henrietta asked.

"I think so."

"Miss James was afraid it might hurt her pride," Henrietta said.

"She doesn't know how to let people . . . help her," Karen said bleakly.

Poor Karen, she seemed on the edge of other people's lives rather than in the center of her own. In some ways she seemed younger than Red, who did know her own mind, a little more than was wise perhaps. It was hard for these young women, who either wouldn't or couldn't take the ordinary ways out, who had instead to make lives for themselves. Henrietta did not envy them.

The news of Karen's own legacy did not send her running in protest out of her cottage. She was under no misapprehension that her mother had wanted to die for Karen's sake. But the lawyer's letter did confuse and depress her. She could not put it away in the ugly handbag stuffed with jewelry and try to forget it. Within a few months she would have two hundred thousand dollars to do with what she saw fit. How puny it made her own year's savings of which she had begun to grow proud. It was not the whole of her mother's estate. The rest of it had been left to her father. She wondered if he would feel minimized by it, too. Had her mother's money been responsible for the kind of house they had lived in, her father's expensive cars? It had certainly been responsible for her mother's running away. Without it, she couldn't have left.

"I don't need it," Karen said aloud. "I don't want it."

"Give it away then," she answered herself.

"Dad would have me committed!" she protested.

Karen had no idea what to do with unnecessary money but put it in the bank until there was enough to buy something. She was still so new at saving that she hadn't had to make any real decisions. Up to now, she'd had fantasies rather than plans. Buying a house had been years in the future. Even buying some few things of her own, pots and pans, dishes, she hadn't seriously thought about. Her only substantial possession, her car, had been given to her by her father, and he paid the insurance.

Now in a few months, if she wanted to, she could buy a little house and furnish it, not because someone had loved her and wanted her to have it though. How angry she had been at Red, and it was an anger fed with envy, that she could be given Miss James' house and not want it, then turn it over almost casually to Karen as if it really weren't worth having.

Red had changed. From someone who needed to learn things and was willing to ask, she was all of a sudden deaf to any advice, and bossy. The dog was nearly as bad, growling at Karen when she got anywhere close to the baby unless Red told her it was all right. Karen wanted to say to them both, "Have your precious baby. I don't want to smell it or to baby-sit."

Karen had never liked children, and this creature seemed no more than an open-ended digestive tract. The best Karen could do was to imagine that she might like it well enough when it was toilet-trained and could walk and talk.

She supposed that must be how a good many men felt, and she was newly admiring of a man like Rat who had conquered such a natural aversion and tended his own child, who was old enough now to begin to look human, hair on his head, a recognizable smile.

It startled her that such a small thing could rouse such strong emotion in her, nearly like jealousy. But anything that suddenly became the whole focus of someone's life was bound to be resented. You weren't supposed to talk to Red when the baby was nursing. You weren't supposed to speak above a whisper when she was asleep, but the stupid dog could put a wet nose right on her, no matter what it had been sniffing five minutes before.

Karen was being unreasonable. She knew that. But she had worked hard to be Red's friend and had begun to think Red cared for her a little, too. And Red did. She'd offered her the house. But their relationship had changed. Red was suddenly in charge and doing her favors. Karen had imagined that Red would be more vulnerable and open when she had the baby. Instead she had become a Landowner and a Mother.

Last night in the pub, for the first time Karen hadn't retreated when Milly said Miss High-and-Mighty wasn't issuing invitations yet to view the Royal Child.

"Just go," Rat had said. "That's what everyone else is doing."

Milly had, after all, given Red the cradle. The least she could do was ask Milly over. But Red had no manners.

"You wanted her to want you," Karen said firmly. "And she doesn't. She's never wanted anything but that baby."

"Did I really want her?" Karen asked herself.

"Yes, no. I just wanted, and she was there."

Karen got up and walked out onto her deck, restless and ashamed of herself. She looked out on a view that could now absorb and soothe her, a modest accomplishment for a year's living here, but a real one. She could be alone. And soon she'd have to tell the owners whether or not she'd be back in September. This might be one of her last days here.

It was time to go over to Miss James' house where Henrietta had promised to help her sort out whatever Red wouldn't need or want. Red wouldn't discuss it. She just would not put her mind to the fact that everything in the house was hers.

Karen arrived early and had the cardboard boxes from the store stacked on the porch waiting for Henrietta who had the key to the new padlock.

"I'm sorry I'm late," Henrietta called. "Everything seems to take me twice as long as it used to. I don't know how I'd ever manage to catch a ferry."

"Do you need help at your house," Karen asked, "until Red comes back?"

"Oh, not really, child," Henrietta said. "I can manage."

Was she aware of taking up Miss James' way of address? Karen at that moment didn't mind being called "child"; she even felt gently claimed by it.

They had no trouble with the clothes. There were not a great many, and they all seemed to be clean. They could be boxed and sent to the thrift shop. When they'd emptied the closets and drawers, Karen took the vacuum to them while Henrietta cut fresh paper for lining.

"It will be a while before the smell of her sachets is gone," Henrietta said. "It's not something people do much anymore. Even my mother's dollar bills smelled of her perfume."

"I wonder what Red will do with this jewelry," Karen said, looking into the dressing table drawer.

The contents looked oddly like the things her

mother had sent to her, probably because Miss James had collected it in her travels too — ethnic junk rather than love tokens.

"Would you like any of it?" Henrietta asked.

"Oh, no," Karen said, withdrawing.

"Well, we certainly can leave some things up to Red," Henrietta decided.

In the bathroom she insisted on throwing out all the medicines, even the aspirin, and she directed Karen to sort through the towels for any that were badly worn. Underneath the towels, Karen found an ancient bathing suit about which they laughed. Then Karen started on the supply shelf.

"Red won't have to buy toilet paper for years," she said.

As she moved the rolls to be sure nothing was hidden behind them, one toppled over and revealed a stash of paper money at its hollow center.

"Look at this!" Karen exclaimed.

They counted five hundred dollars.

"What a place to keep money!" Henrietta exclaimed. "I imagine it's the sort of thing Red does with her own. She's simply going to have to open a bank account now."

When they finally arrived at the kitchen, Henrietta proposed a break. She sat down so gratefully that Karen realized she was too tired for more. Karen made them tea, her first domestic act in this house.

"The kitchen ought to be pretty straightforward," Karen said. "I can do that when I move in."

"You might just remember to move any of the cleaning things or poisons out of the way of a baby while you're at it," Henrietta suggested.

"Isn't Red lucky?" Karen said wistfully as she sipped her tea from a thin china cup.

"I hope so," Henrietta said.

"Rat advised me not to wait for an invitation," Milly said, standing at Red's door.

"I don't invite people," Red said. "Now they just come."

"Well, that's good," Milly said. "I see I'm not the only one to think of Pampers."

There were boxes of disposable diapers piled neatly against the wall. The baby slept in the cradle on a luxuriant lambskin surrounded by stuffed animals, most of them locally made. And there were stacks of baby clothes on the few available surfaces.

"I could just about open a store," Red said, looking around.

"That's the island," Milly said. "Whether your house burns down or you have a baby, the goods pile in. And after all, it's Dickie's child."

"She's a third-generation islander," Red agreed complacently.

Milly walked over to the cradle to look at Blue, too small still to claim likenesses, but when she did, Red wouldn't object. This strange, rootless girl had managed a pedigree for her bastard child, and obviously no one but its own grandmother was going to deny it.

"Has Sadie come?" Milly asked.

"We don't need her," Red said.

"I shouldn't think you do," Milly agreed. "Let's

just hope Blue hasn't inherited Sadie's love of the bottle."

"People have choices about things like that," Red answered.

So Red had thought about that, too, calculating all the odds. Blue could use some of Dickie's good looks. And he hadn't lacked brains; he'd chosen to be stupid.

"People who grow up here and don't know anything else sometimes don't realize what their choices are," Milly said.

"That happens anywhere," Red said.

"So how are you?" Milly asked, giving Red an evaluating look.

"I'm all right, but I've decided not to come back to work until September."

"I guess that won't kill me," Milly decided. "When are you going to move?"

"September, probably," Red said.

"That's going to be a change," Milly said, looking around. "Surprised me, Miss James did."

Red's face had closed, and Milly knew her well enough to recognize the signal and back off. At that moment, Blackie arrived at the door, a low growl starting in her throat.

"It's all right, Blackie," Red said.

Milly laughed.

"She's not used to so many people," Red explained, rubbing one of Blackie's ears.

"You remember about the highchair when she's ready for it," Milly said.

"Thanks."

Milly walked back up the road relieved to have

seen the baby and satisfied her curiosity about the way Red lived. Milly would certainly never have wanted to raise a child, children, alone. She would never have lived alone by choice. And to live that poor, like somebody out of a past century — Milly was sure she would have taken to the streets before she did that. Nothing was a real choice for a woman unless dictating among disasters counted. Maybe being alone wasn't so difficult if you'd never been happy.

"Certainly I've been happy," Milly said to herself as she got into her car.

Stuck behind a family of cyclists, the youngest no more than five, wobbling and weaving along behind the others, Milly dawdled along until there was a safe stretch of road to pass. Islanders cursed this summer traffic, and Milly did, too, but she liked the summer, remembering her own children on bicycles coming down the hill toward her like a flock of birds.

Chapter XVI

"Miss James is not going to just disappear," Karen said with nervous firmness to Red's silence on the other end of the phone. "Red?"

"I'm listening," Red replied softly. "I don't want to wake Blue."

"Well, I'm sorry," Karen said impatiently, "but either she's awake so you can't talk or she's asleep so you can't talk."

There was no reply.

"With no funeral, with no memorial, Miss James

doesn't just go away," Karen tried to explain. "Getting rid of her clothes didn't help."

"What do you want to do?" Red asked.

"Exorcise her," Karen replied.

"I don't know what that means."

"We have to do something to let her — or anyway this house — know she's dead."

"Don't you want to stay there?" Red asked.

"I do . . . if I can," Karen said. "But it's your problem, too, Red. I can't do it by myself."

"Can't you ask Mrs. Hawkins?"

"Hen didn't inherit this house. You did."

"I know, and I'll deal with it. I really will when I can."

"Listen, Red, if I give a sort of party, would you at least come to it?"

"I guess so," Red said, "if I can."

Karen hung up, disgusted.

"Well, what do you think of her now?" Karen demanded.

In the two days since she'd moved in, Karen had stopped talking to herself and addressed all her remarks to Miss James whose spirit in this house was too lively to seem like a ghost.

"You're meant to be her problem, not mine."

The house was so clearly designed for one person that trying to live in it without taking Miss James' place left no comfortable place to be. Other chairs in the living room were adequate only if you didn't want to read or watch TV. Even in the kitchen Miss James' chair was the only convenient one if you were waiting on yourself. But whenever Karen tried to assert herself, to take Miss James' place, she was filled with restless apprehension.

Karen was grateful Miss James had not died in her bed, but she herself had not slept well in it for the past two nights, waking often with the peculiar sensation that she was trapped in someone else's skin.

None of the strategies she'd developed for living alone seemed to work in this house. She found herself reverting to all the tricks she had learned to avoid going home. She couldn't believe that this might happen to her again wherever she went. That would be simply too discouraging.

Red obviously didn't know what Karen was talking about. Maybe by the time Red moved in, it would be all right, or she'd be too preoccupied and insensitive to notice. She had no trouble nursing a dead man's baby. Maybe she could live comfortably in a dead woman's house.

Karen wondered why she'd ever thought she could make friends with Red. It wasn't just that Red's vocabulary was so limited that she couldn't understand half of what Karen said; Red didn't care. But then, who did?

"How could you live all those years," Karen demanded, "like this?"

Was she really asking Miss James, or her mother? Neither would answer her, and perhaps she was a little crazy, having slipped first into talking to herself and now slipping further into talking with the dead. At least when she talked to herself, she responded.

Answer me! she wanted to shout but instead rushed out of the house and down across the road to the sea. She stood watching the pleasure boats anchored out by the point. She hadn't once been fishing. Adam had asked her, but she couldn't have

227

made friends with him. That wasn't what he'd have wanted. Now that the pub was full of summer people, he hardly bothered to speak to her.

Why was she suddenly so angry with everyone, the dead as well as the living?

"I'm sick of this place," she said aloud.

"Then move on," she answered.

Oddly there was no blank wall of WHERE before her but an open, even inviting, horizon. She didn't feel afraid.

Karen walked back up to the house, went in and sat down at Miss James' desk. She had cleared it of everything personal, but Miss James' scent still clung to the blank stationery. Karen took out four sheets and began to make signs for the island's billboards. *You are invited to share memories and thoughts of Miss James at her house on Friday at 7:30 p.m.* She paused, considering, then printed *Karen Tasuki*. Let them say it wasn't her place to do it. Let them decide not to come.

"I've got to make it my place until I leave," she said to Miss James, who seemed a little more willing to share her desk than she had been.

Now Karen had things to do to get ready for the party that might or might not take place. She baked a modest number of cookies, bought a few cold cuts and some cheese, a half a dozen bottles of wine, and arranged to borrow the smallest coffee maker from the hall, as well as cups and glasses.

In the three days she prepared, no one mentioned her signs to her, and no one called to offer help. Perhaps they expected her to ask for it. She didn't need any.

On Friday afternoon, when she'd finished her

duties at the ferry dock, she went home and began to make a small number of sushi.

"Why not one last one in the eye for silly Milly Forbes?" she asked Miss James or herself; they both agreed.

Adam, if he came, actually liked sushi. For a wistful moment, she admitted to herself that she wanted him to come, and Riley and Rat and his wife, Homer and Jane, all of them. But she stopped that hope by concentrating on what she was doing.

In the middle of her task, it came to her that what she really wanted to do was learn Japanese. Why? Did she have to have a reason? Then she had one. She wanted to be able to read that gravestone she had so rashly claimed for her great-grandfather. If she wanted to learn Japanese, why not go to Japan? She would be little more of a stranger there than she was here. Her father would be appalled. Well, as he said himself, she was a grown woman. And she could afford it.

For the first time, her inheritance from her mother occurred to her as a blessing. She was, after all, free to make her own terms with the world. Why on earth had she been hanging around the edges of other people's lives when she had her own? Here she was in Red's house, envying Red's good fortune, even taking on what she thought of as Red's responsibilities when she could be on her way to Japan. The world out there beyond this little island was full of people, among whom there might be someone she could risk wanting on her own terms.

At seven o'clock, Red arrived, the baby asleep in a carrier on her breast, in her hand a basket full of things for the baby, on top of which was a pie.

"I couldn't get here any earlier," Red said. "I don't seem to be as well organized as I thought."

"I didn't expect you to help," Karen said, too relieved to see her to leave room for grievance.

Red looked around at the food and drink.

"It sure looks different," she said.

"It's beginning to feel that way, too," Karen agreed.

"Is it okay if I put Blue on . . . your bed?" Red asked.

"It's Miss James' or yours," Karen said. "I just sleep there."

"Karen, I'm sorry you're mad at me. I wish I could be your friend, but I can't now. I don't know how. It's something maybe I'll never learn."

Karen looked at Red, so lately in the bloom of pregnancy, now white and drawn with all the new demands being made on her, and wondered at her own anger. "You are my friend and a good one," Karen admitted. "I haven't any business being mad at you. I'm sorry."

Milly sat at the desk which had been Forbes', finishing a letter she had promised to write to Bonnie. Writing was far easier than she had expected, not only because it didn't have to be a performance for everyone else on the party line but also because she felt so much closer to Bonnie since she'd been here. Milly's sense of mortal power over her daughter had faded considerably, but her affection for her had not, nourished as it was more and more often by memories of her as a child, memories of all the children in those long sunny summers here on the island. She could recall to Bonnie a remark she'd made when she was around twelve: "I'm so glad, Mother, you don't make jelly and pies. We get to eat all the berries we pick." There had been a time when her children had approved of her. Though Bonnie certainly had her reservations now, Milly sensed that she was now more in her daughter's good graces than she had been for some years.

When she had finished the letter, she sat for some time, thinking not of Bonnie but of Nora, the daughter lost to her whose blue eyes could be as cold as her own. Yet she had been there in Milly's memories with Martin and Bonnie, Nora their leader always, the brightest and bravest of the lot, and Forbes' favorite, Milly had always suspected. Though he had been a fair father, she had to give him that. How had they managed these things so badly that they'd lost a child in the process? And was she really lost? Nobody had made any real attempt to find her.

Dear Forbes, Milly wrote. *This isn't a request for money; so don't throw it away before you read it.*

She was tempted first to blame him once again, but they'd both been disgusting. All she really wanted now was to offer Nora a chance to forgive them.

Please find Nora, she wrote. *It's time.*

When she addressed that letter, she went to her closet to look for something appropriate among her summer things for a memorial evening. As she looked, she thought how much too young as well as too shabby and too small her clothes were for her. By now she hadn't much idea what fashions were. And what difference did it really make? She took out a wraparound navy skirt and the freshest-looking of her white blouses. If she was beginning to look more and more like a real islander, why not? There were worse things to be.

As she picked up the platter of raw vegetables and dip she was taking, she wondered how old she'd have to be before she could get away with coffee or tea bags.

Henrietta was not waiting at the end of her drive as she had done before Hart died. She was waiting at her door and came slowly and tentatively to the car carrying a plate of sandwiches.

"I couldn't face the oven on so hot a day," she confessed.

"Do you feel a bit funny about this?" Milly couldn't resist asking.

"No, why?"

"Well, it just doesn't seem to me her place to do it."

"I don't know why not," Henrietta said. "She's living there now, and Red's too busy with the baby to take it on. Oh, I feel a bit guilty, to tell the truth, but then I thought how nice that a young person would think of it and do it."

"Did she ask you to bring something?" Milly asked.

"No. But I thought she's probably too shy to."

"Well, when I go, I hope my memorial won't be announced on the bulletin boards like a washing machine for sale."

"It's a way to make sure everybody's welcome," Henrietta said. "I think Miss James would have liked it."

"Whatever happens, this time I'm not taking Sadie home," Milly determined.

"I don't think she'll be there somehow. She didn't even want to go to Dickie's funeral."

"And she wants nothing to do with that baby. She thinks of it as Dickie's revenge."

"Just as well," Henrietta said. "Red really isn't interested in sharing that baby with anyone."

"Except the dog," Milly said.

Henrietta laughed.

Milly glanced over at her to catch sight of that vitality which would now only occasionally rise into Henrietta's face. Henrietta was too old to recover completely. Milly liked her better, being able to feel always a little sorry for her. And Milly was particularly glad of her company as they walked through Miss James' wildflower garden because alone Milly would have felt far from sure of welcome. The only way this invitation could include her was on a bulletin board.

Miss James' small house was already crowded, and Milly was surprised at the number of young people there. She'd never had the impression that Miss James had much to do with the young, except for her dependence on and attachment to Red. Were they this hard up for a party?

"Would you like wine or tea or coffee?" Karen asked her.

"Wine, thank you," Milly replied, relieved to be able to respond just as she would at the pub.

"Try one of these, Milly," Adam said, holding out a plate of sushi.

"Thank you, no," Milly said, sweeping past him into the living room.

Henrietta, watching her go, gave Karen a rueful

smile at the same moment Adam and Karen burst out laughing, obvious conspirators in a private joke.

"Excuse me, Hen," Karen said. "What can I get for you?"

"A place to sit down," Henrietta confessed. "I'm no good at standing."

All the chairs in the living room, except Miss James' own, had been taken. Henrietta hesitated for only a moment before she moved to it and sat down, thinking herself as likely a candidate as any. How substantial and nearly sacred or obscene furniture became when those who had claimed it were dead. This odd game they were playing should be called musical people, for at each gathering one more was gone while the chairs stayed on. A baby's cry from the bedroom reminded Henrietta that there were also those newly born to insure the furniture had its uses, but she had lost too many of her own to take the comfort there should be in each new life.

It was that dwindling interest the young found so hard to forgive. Red couldn't understand why Miss James hadn't at least waited to see the baby, had strained all her will instead against that eventuality. Miss James would have been pleased at the neatness of it, dying the day the baby was born, the one passage actually involved in bringing on the other.

Miss James would have preferred Red to be in charge of the house and the party, but she might have understood Red's need to act in her own way, to take her time. And it was important for Karen, who had been a favorite with Miss James, too, to take just such a place as this in the community.

"It's hard to believe you've been here only just

over a year," Henrietta said to Karen, accepting the glass of wine she offered.

"I'm on my way the end of the month," Karen confided.

"Oh?"

"I've decided to go to Japan," Karen said. "I've never been."

"Well," Henrietta said reluctantly, "perhaps the time for you young people to go is when people begin to take you for granted. We'll miss you."

"Thank you," Karen said and turned away quickly as if the comment had been embarrassing in some way.

Henrietta wasn't used to being lacking in tact. You could only be tactful in a world you paid attention to and understood. She wondered if she'd ever have enough energy or interest to relearn that skill.

Red came over and squatted down by Henrietta.

"I like to see you sitting there," Red said. "It helps."

"Karen says she's leaving us."

"She just decided," Red said. "She was afraid no one would come."

"Why?" Henrietta asked in surprise. "People always do."

"For births and deaths," Red remarked.

"And fires," Henrietta added.

"And fires," Red agreed.

"Has Karen had a hard time living here?" Henrietta asked.

"She tried to make friends with me," Red said.

"And someone has to be pretty hard up to try a thing like that? Oh, Red!"

"I'm not ready to be a friend," Red said. "And maybe I never will be."

"Having a baby is a pretty big responsibility. Friends can help," Henrietta said.

"They don't," Red said. "They get in the way."

"Oh, I know they can," Henrietta said, a sudden memory of herself frantically trying to protect her first living baby from the hordes of gift-bearing visitors, and she was naturally sociable, not a cautious hermit like Red.

Homer and Jane had arrived, and Red rose to greet them, a gesture which suggested she might be reluctantly practicing for the time she would be mistress of this house. Henrietta couldn't imagine another gathering such as this at Red's instigation. But Blue had already changed Red's relationship to the community, and, as the human traffic died down, she would suspect and resent it less and only gradually know she'd been a little changed by it, more open to human connection than she could now imagine.

In the absence of Sadie, the young men were paying some court to Milly who looked remarkably well, her face no longer such a careful mask of makeup, her body taking its fuller, more natural shape. She was making them laugh.

Karen came to Henrietta and asked, "Do you think it's time that we maybe said a little bit about Miss James?"

"Yes," Henrietta said.

Karen tapped her glass until the room was quiet.

"I didn't ask anyone ahead of time to make a speech, but I thought maybe now anyone who wanted to say something could. I've only known Miss James

— and all of you — for a bit more than a year, but I learned a lot from her, maybe mostly about living alone. She did it so well I began to think I might learn to like it. I still don't, but I can do it."

There was an amused murmur.

"She talked a lot about her travels. One of her teacups or a picture could start her off, and maybe part of the secret of living alone well is collecting a lot of good memories. She had the courage to do that. The first brave thing I ever did in my life was moving to this island. The next bravest thing I'm going to do is go to Japan."

"One day," Riley said, "when I gave her a lift into town, she had me nearly talked into going to Alaska, and I still think maybe some day I'll make it."

"Miss James," said Henrietta from Miss James' chair, "would have had a poem to recite."

Everyone nodded.

"She was a good, wise friend to me. I'm going to miss her very much," Henrietta concluded.

That simplicity encouraged others without confidence in their eloquence to share an anecdote or a bit of homely philosophy, letting short silences fall between speakers without any sense of embarrassment. It was a ritual they understood.

Finally Red stepped forward and said, "I've memorized a poem Miss James liked. It's called 'Rumination' by Richard Eberhart.

> When I can hold a stone within my hand
> And feel time make it sand and soil, and see
> The roots of living things grow in this land,
> Pushing between my fingers flower and tree,

Then I shall be as wise as death,
For death has done this and he will
Do this to me, and blow his breath
To fire my clay, when I am still."

"Thank you, Red," Henrietta said.

It was about Hart's roses, she supposed, or her own lilies, living consolations against the rebuking furniture. Miss James went on reading poetry far too long in order to keep sharing it with the young who might need to think death was wise instead of simply mindless.

"This is also now a house-warming," Karen said, holding up a new bottle of wine, "for Red."